HONOR IN AN AGE OF METAL AND MEN

ANTHONY W. EICHENLAUB

To Dad: always the teacher, always the hero.
A truer man of honor I have never known.

1

———

Some folks claimed the world ended the day Texas became everything. When the earth shook from the Yellowstone supervolcano and America tumbled back into the vast void of history, only stubborn Texas held itself together—and indeed expanded its reach—with razor claws and steel-corded muscle. The years of ash and storm failed to end the tech-drenched state of Texas, but there was one thing left to hold a threat to the Lone Star.

Texas itself.

War raged across the land in the form of a thousand battles on a thousand lines. Robots threatened cars in the sky and swarms of drones threatened fragile infrastructure. In the years after the start of the Second Civil War, rebels scattered to the corners, hiding from Austin's massive reach. They fought Austin's oppressive iron fist in the streets of every small town and atop every hill, but nobody ever won.

There I was, sitting at the northern edge of Texas, where the grit of the Colorado wastes butted up against the foot of the Yellowstone Mountains. Every soul around would say this wasn't part of Texas. They'd call it a Navajo Nation or the free country. They might be right, but far as I was concerned that place still held the red-hot glowing soul of Texas.

At the foot of that monstrous mountain range, where the Yellowstone Caldera still smoldered with sulfurous ash, Texans did what Texans did best.

They played football on a Friday night.

"It ain't what it used to be, J.D.," said Pa. He sat next to me, shriveled in his black leather coat. The old man still wore the gambler hat that was his signature back when he was bounty hunting. The breath that wafted over his black teeth smelled of cheap beer and jalapeños. "Kids used to be tough."

Down on the field, the play started. The blue team, some small contingent of Navajo and Hopi, hiked the ball and ran up the middle only to be stopped hard by a left tackle the size of a small rhino.

"Displacement rules saved the sport," I said, my heart not in the argument, which we'd had a thousand times. "Kids were getting killed or modified beyond reason." I looked down at the huge three-fingered monstrosity that I called a left hand. It hadn't been my choice to get the modification, but the thing came in handy from time to time. I hardly remembered who I was without it. "They're in high school, Pa. They don't need this crap."

"Don't need it?" Pa waved a hand in front of his face, as if swatting away flies. "Every damn one of these kids leaves high school better off."

"If they survive."

The blue team hiked second down, running the same damn play. Again, the big guy with the ten-yard reach stopped their runner. Most Navajo refused to resort to human modification to enhance their players. It was part of why they rarely won.

I shifted my ass on the bleacher. The stadium wasn't a large one, and it wasn't full. Across the field only a couple hundred people cheered for the other side. Pa and I sat on the much busier half, but this far north the teams rarely drew a sellout crowd. Somewhere, meat charred on a fire, and a smoky haze filled the bowl of the stadium.

Blue lined up again, squared solidly, bravely, against the red and orange of some nearby town. Tension built in the stands like a clenched fist. This was third and ten, end of the fourth with a tied score. The kids on the field stood tall and squat alike, some with gangling, grasping arms, others with solid, tense muscle. The displacement rules didn't limit them to a weight class, but limited the amount of water each kid displaced. So, the big kids were huge and light. The smaller kids dense and unstoppable.

What it all came down to was that some teams played smart and some teams played hard.

The blue Navajo team—the local team—played smart. They had big kids. Some huge. They had smaller kids—hard to avoid in a small town. It was number nine on the blue team that made a difference. He wasn't big, but that quarterback played smart and moved fast. He called a timeout with seconds to go. They'd have one last play.

Pa was talking, but I tuned him out until he said, "J.D., sometimes you need to pick your bounties, and this one just isn't worth it."

"What do you know about my bounty?"

I was a bounty hunter, fallen a hell of a long way from sheriff of Dead Oak, Texas. Hell, I half expected a posse to roll around and lock me up, based on my previous dealings with the law. If Sheriff Trish didn't do it, then someone from Austin had my number, sure as could be.

"I know plenty," Pa said. He took a deep swig of clear beer. "I know it's a double warrant. Two bounties out for the same guy is sometimes good, son, but when one wants him dead and one wants him alive, there's trouble all over it."

"You talking about the warrant for Francis Brown? What makes you think I'm taking it?"

Pa shook his head. "You've been chasing that kid since you ran outta Dead Oak. Now someone wants to pay you to find him? Two someones? You'd be a damn fool to pass that up."

"So, you think I should play the fool?"

"Deals this good don't happen." He took another swig. "Deals this good kill hunters stupid enough to go in guns blazing."

"I ain't stupid. I know better than anyone how dangerous he is." My own beer was empty, so I took my Stetson in hand and flagged down a vendor. The new beer was cold, but everything tasted of sulfur and grit that far north into the wastelands. "And I'm a good shot. A decent marksman's only gotta blaze once to get the job done."

Pa shushed me and leaned forward in his seat. The blue team lined up again, and the play was fixing to start. Number nine brought them out with the exact same lineup, with everybody in the same positions.

"What the hell?" I muttered. Around me, the rest of the crowd had the same sentiment. They'd run this twice. What did that kid have to prove?

Everything, it turned out. The center hiked the ball and ran up the middle, but everything went different. This time, in a collision of muscle and metal, plastic and sweat, the blue team hit in a coordinated wedge, driving under the giant player. They lifted him and tossed him aside like so much beef. The quarterback ran straight under the big kid, straight into the vacated space.

Ten, twenty. The other team fought to recover. The long-legged runners, with their lanky, grasping arms, pivoted too late. The blue runner was past them. Thirty. Forty. The clock ran out.

Touchdown!

The crowd exploded into cheers. Horns blared and fire-works shot into the sky.

When the applause subsided, I asked, "What makes you so sure I'm going to take that job?"

"Because you've already taken it."

I looked at the old man for a long time. He'd shrunken as he aged, but he was still as fierce as a firecracker. Pa didn't dance around something unless he felt it was worth dancing around. He didn't interfere in my work unless he thought it needed interfering.

"Where is he?" I asked.

A black-toothed smile spread across his face. "'Bout seven rows back, and he's been there all game." He touched the rim of his round hat. "I take that back. He's just slipped out the back."

"Aw, hell," I stood.

Pa grasped my wrist. "Son," he said.

"I gotta do this, Pa. He's murdered hundreds all over Texas."

"That ain't it."

He was right. Francis William Brown had murdered the man I loved. In that one strike, all those years ago, he'd done me in. "You always taught me to never walk away when honor's at stake."

His knobby-knuckled grip eased. "Sure," he said. "Sure. Do what you need to do." There was more resignation in his voice than was warranted.

I smoothed my duster—a high-tech thing made to shrug off bullets and fire. Every time I put it on I wished Zane were with me—a painful reminder of our short time together. I kept the duster because it kept me safe. As a bounty hunter, I needed it—especially now.

Francis couldn't have gone far. While the crowd still cheered the Navajo victory, I exited through the nearest tunnel to the back of the stadium. Taking two steps at a time brought me through a concrete arch decorated with the Navajo symbols of the team: the crow, the coyote, and the peace pipe. The art was crude, painted no doubt by the same kids who fought on the field below.

The stadium itself sat in the crotch of two massive lava flows. The black rock rose up on either side, long since cooled and hardened into impenetrable walls. That left only one way for Francis to run if he were attempting to escape.

But I didn't think he was.

"Why are you here?" I muttered.

Pa had been right. I had invited the old man to that game on this Friday because my sources had hinted Francis would be there. My criminal contacts were about as reliable as a pronghorn in a dust storm, but they were all I had. The opportunity to spend a little time with Pa hadn't been something I could pass up. Age makes us faded versions of ourselves, and when men fade, it's best to spend time when the opportunity arises.

My own bones weren't feeling particularly young. Under my Stetson, my hair had gone all gray and I'd chopped it short. I'd slowed over the years, and a paunch of a belly had grown to show for it. A man can't be too concerned about such things. My one blind eye, where the tech had long since failed, hardly bothered me anymore, and the grinding of my ancient metal arm didn't hardly keep me awake anymore. It was what it was.

Several horses were tied behind the stadium where a posted deputy guarded against thieves. Muffin was tied there, and with a nod to the deputy, I untied her. She was tall and black, sleekly muscular, and gorgeous as gorgeous gets. When I placed a hand on her neck, she leaned into me as if she'd missed my touch. I sure as hell had missed hers. I mounted up and led her down the path away from the mountain and the stadium.

No sign of Francis. If he'd run fast, he might have made it down the one rocky road, but I still didn't think he was running. Hell, if he'd run there wasn't much chance I'd catch him. Best assume he was still around the stadium. I urged Muffin back up the slope.

Movement. At the edge of the concessions stand. A flash of metal and a quickness that triggered an old sheriff's instinct. This was the movement of someone trying not to be seen. Francis.

"Yah!" Muffin closed the distance fast at my urging. She circled around the stand—nothing more than a squat wooden structure—and I saw the running man making his way along the outside of the stadium. I followed.

By the time we caught up, the man had scrambled up the slope of black rock. He darted across the uneven surface, and when he shot a cold glance back my way I recognized Francis Brown. His eyes glowed an eerie violet, more than just a reflection of the stadium's nighttime illumination. He had sallow cheekbones and long, stringy hair that fell across his weather-hardened face like a waterfall in a drought.

"Crow," he shouted. His voice came out flat, but a click in the back of his throat hinted at emotion. "Been a while."

Not wanting to injure Muffin on the slope, I dismounted and climbed after Francis. "You're coming with me, Francis."

Francis pulled himself up another low ridge.

Black rock bit into my knuckles as I climbed, but my metal arm pulled me up, launching me after Francis.

He ran across a flat flow of black rock. I sprinted, sweating in the autumn heat. It'd take one shot to drop that man, one bullet to finish this bounty, but I couldn't shoot a man in the back. Honor wouldn't let me.

I gained on him. Age had ruined my body, but inactivity had slowed his. He leapt over a gap, landing hard on the other side. I jumped after him.

It was a whole hell of a lot longer than I expected. A crack in the black rock gaped below me, and time slowed when I saw that my feet weren't anywhere near going to land on solid ground. Francis watched me hit the ledge, no apparent emotion on his face. He watched the way a zookeeper observes a lion eating a steak.

He'd underestimated me. I hit the ridge hard, my black metal hand gripping the ledge above. Instead of hanging there like an idiot, I launched myself up and out, grabbing his shirt with my human hand. Carrying my momentum forward, I shoved him up and back, slamming him hard against the rock. He clawed at my hand in an attempt to get free.

I got my face up close to his. "What are you doing here, boy?"

His expression didn't change. "There are two bounties out on me."

Switching hands so that I gripped his whole chest with my big metal hand, I drew my weapon. Blood dripped from my hand where he'd gouged deep into the flesh, but I ignored the pain. "One dead," I said. "One alive."

He coughed. "Which one are you going to pick?"

My jaw tensed. "Figure I'll try one, then the other," I said. "Starting with dead."

I jammed the revolver up against his jaw. I had one bullet for him, a Red Number Five that would punch through whatever armor he'd bothered to integrate with that pale skin of his. It could end just like this: the pain, the grief, the raw hole where justice used to live. Pull the trigger and this monster of a man would be dead. The thought sent ice through my veins.

"Why'd you come here?" I growled.

"For me," said a girl's voice behind me.

The kid standing on the other side of the chasm had dark tan skin seared by a life in the desert sun. That and her long black hair hinted at Navajo, but guessing heritage was an iffy thing. Most wouldn't spot the drop of Hopi blood in my own veins. This kid was slight of build and had a spark in her eyes. She wore the blue jersey of the football team I'd just watched win against those monstrous modders. Number nine. She was the quarterback. She smiled at me with white teeth as if she were in on some secret joke.

Francis twitched and I cracked him hard on the head. He slumped. "Who the hell are you?" I asked the newcomer.

"Quin," she said. She nodded at Francis. "And that asshole is my ticket out of here."

"Well," I said, "you're going to want to find another ride." I hefted Francis's unconscious form over my shoulder and walked away.

2

———

I couldn't take Francis back over the pit, since the jump would be too much. Instead, I walked the long way around, farther upslope until the rocky ridge of black stone arched back down to meet with the old soil among the dead trees. All the while, I carried Francis over my left shoulder.

Quin disappeared, probably too clever to jump the chasm that had nearly killed me. When I reached a branch in the ridge, more mountain towered above me to the north. The rock blotted out the night sky, like a black behemoth swallowing the whole universe. Spotting a fair enough path back, I scrambled forward. Sweat poured from me, and my breaths came in raspy gulps. This wasn't the kind of work I'd ever enjoyed, and in my current shape it wasn't something I was sure I would even survive.

Francis stirred, so I hurried down the mountain. My boots held poor purchase on the warm rock, but I managed to reach soil before the man woke. The scratch on my hand still oozed blood and ached something fierce, so I bandaged it as best I could. It got nowhere near clean, but the nanomachines in my blood would fight infection well enough. Hell, they'd fight anything that came close and knit me back together. It had been a long time since I'd worried about superficial wounds like that.

By the time he opened his eyes I had a gun leveled at his face. I hadn't bothered with e-cuffs to disable his tech. A man like Francis probably employed all the latest workarounds for standard law-enforcement tech. He stared out beyond me with dull eyes. Fella like that can move worlds with that look. It spoke of a raw, disciplined power and a confidence that he thought he was the one in charge. "I'll come quiet," he said.

"You will."

He blinked. "I don't fancy eating a bullet."

"Word is you can kill a man fast as thinking about it."

A hint of a smile creased the corner of one eye, so subtle it might have been nothing. "I might get control of your arm and that gear in your head," he said, "but not so quick you wouldn't unload that pistol before you died." He closed his eyes. "I promise, I'll come quiet."

I'd never heard him speak anything but lies, but something in his voice gave me a shred of confidence. He was resigned, the way a man with real emotions might resign after a resounding defeat and a fit of depression. After a moment's pause, he struggled to his feat, swaying in the dark night.

"Walk," I said.

He made his way forward, black rock towering on either side of us. Ahead, the dim stadium loomed, silent after all the excitement of the previous hours. Keeping close to the ridge, we eventually found Muffin. I picked up her lead and we continued down, past the stadium. The whole place felt like a disturbed graveyard; the thick scent of human activity clung to vacant lots and moonlit monoliths. How fast the excitement of the Friday night burned away.

"Who is it wants me alive?" Francis asked in a quiet voice.

I almost didn't answer. Wasn't any business of his, after all. "Sheriff Trish Chin wants a little chat."

"Down in Dead Oak? I haven't been down that way in years."

Trish's request had me wondering too. What with the war on and his outlaw status, Francis would have been a fool to have any desire to visit his hometown. "You're mighty popular with the law folk down that way. Always have been."

For a long time he didn't answer. Finally, he said, "I suppose."

We came across the little Navajo town where the football team still celebrated their victory. Kids whooped and hollered, firing guns in the air and drinking trash beer. As kids do. In a barn at the edge of town I found my coffin. It sat partially covered in straw, with shining white sides standing out in sharp contrast to the black night. I brushed it off and pulled it open to reveal the padded interior.

"Get in," I said.

He shot me a look, and for a fraction of a second a shred of worry creased his brow.

"You know what this is. Standard bounty hunting gear. You'll be unconscious, hardware disabled, and neutralized for the whole trip." It was similar to the e-cuff tech, but significantly more—aggressive. It might even stand a chance of working on him. When he didn't move, I said, "It's this one or I find you one made of pine."

He lay down in the coffin.

When I shut it, mechanisms hissed and shifted. The whole thing lifted from the ground, antigrav pulsing unsteadily. The man inside would be subdued into a comatose state, and I'd have time to move him wherever I needed before waking him. The shielding on the coffin kept signals from escaping, so he wouldn't be able to summon help or play any of the hacking tricks that the dangerous criminal Francis William Brown was known for. For the first time since spotting Francis in that football stadium, I relaxed.

I lowered the coffin to the ground and buried my face in my hands. This boy had been my quarry for years, always out of reach. He'd been my greatest failure both as a sheriff and as a human being. Now, this murderer—this monster was in a box.

Only then did I start to worry about how easy it had all been. Francis was the most dangerous criminal in all the waste, so why had he come without so much as a fight? As a kid he had learned how to brainwash folks who had sensory input augments. Patches had rolled out since that time, but he was a clever kid. If he had tried, he could have killed me on that mountain.

Why was he in that coffin, dead to the world and prepped for transport?

I sat on the straw next to the coffin, pulled my hat down over my head, and napped. Did no good leaving town in the middle of the night. We had a long walk ahead, and now that Francis was in the box, there wasn't much could go wrong.

When I woke, plenty had gone wrong. Quin, the football player, sat on top of Francis's coffin, legs and arms crossed. A leather satchel sat next to her, and she'd dressed in a woven gray poncho with black silk embroidering the edges. A shotgun rested across her legs.

She looked at me, dark eyes laughing. "Finally. Can we leave now?"

I put on my best scowl, the one that frightens grown men.

Quin thumped the coffin twice, unfazed. "I had a deal with this guy. I've already paid, so unless you want to open this up and get me my money back, I'm coming with."

"Now look—"

"A deal's a deal, right? I mean, I'll get back what's owed me if I have to go talk to the chief, but that doesn't really do me any good."

"Why do you want to leave?"

She shrugged. "It's not really your business, is it?"

"It is if you're an underage kid and your tribe comes hunting for you."

Her expression went dark. "I'm not. They won't."

I smelled bullshit. Hell, I smelled a whole truckload of it. Without any more protest, I readied Muffin for the long walk, brushing her down and getting her saddle on. She was a strong horse, still in her prime. She'd put a lot of kilometers on without any real struggle. When I'd finished, I tied the coffin to the saddle and triggered its antigrav. The box floated with Quin still on top. Quin watched me through all this, eyes taking in all the details of my morning routine.

When I was finished, we left. Quin still sat on the coffin, legs crossed.

The little Navajo town wasn't much more than a cluster of new buildings mixed with the ruins of an old Colorado mining town. Where the new mountains of the Yellowstone Wastes mixed with the old purple mountains of old, life didn't thrive, but it managed. Old men watched from their stoops as I walked Muffin out of town. Children ran through the street, playing games and reenacting the previous night's violent football game. Not a single person bid goodbye to Quin.

Parts of the road were still paved, but we took the smaller paths. Tiny ruts through the mountains, amongst the burned-out forests and acidic soil. Trees were like dark claws grasping for the cold sun, with only the scrubby growths close to the earth making any real attempt at life. It was a dead land, but the farther out of the mountains we traveled, the greener things became.

Around midday, Quin spoke for the first time. "We're being followed."

I grunted my acknowledgement.

We continued down the hill, and after a while, I stopped where our path crossed the once-paved road. There was an overlook, where the people of a long-dead world had decided to designate a beautiful view. They'd paved it over, constructed signs and statues, and generally ruined the whole effect as best they could. We sat there while Muffin grazed on some scrubby grass a short distance away.

Quin had her own food, so I didn't offer mine. All I had was hard bread and some cold oatmeal—anyway, nothing compared to the prepackaged protein bars Quin had brought.

"It's beautiful out here," Quin said. "It's almost like nothing ever went wrong."

The mountains before us glowed in the afternoon sun. Blue-gray peaks reached for the gray-blue skies, mingling with the hazy clouds of the summer afternoon. The air no longer smelled of the sulfurous wastes and had almost lost the burned ash of the ruined forests. It was a pleasant enough afternoon, and the old Americans had been right about that spot. The view was incredible.

"Do you ever wonder what life might have been like before Yellowstone?" Quin asked. "Do you think people came here all the time?"

"They'd be fools not to." I leaned back on the crumbled column that named each of the peaks. "What are you running from?"

Her brow furrowed. "I don't run from nothing."

"Then who's following us?"

"How should I know?"

I shot her a side-eye glance. "You said someone's following us. How do you know?"

She shifted uncomfortably on the still-floating coffin. "I just know."

Pulling out my data cube, I scrolled through options until I found a faint signal. No alerts. No messages. That's what it always looked like for me, but that was the benefit of not having many friends. I checked the job listing and located the bounty for Francis Brown. It was still there, glowing red to indicate that the man was still out there and still dangerous. There was a place in the listing where hunters could claim a job so we'd know if there was competition. My name was at the top of the list, since I'd added it before taking Pa to the football game. It was an honor system, but one that bounty hunters tended to respect.

Below that were two other names: Sunset and Casket Jones.

Shit.

"Well," I said. "Looks like your friend is popular."

Quin laid a hand on her shotgun.

I whistled for Muffin, whose ears perked up. She didn't come or anything, but she knew damn well I wanted her to. That's a horse for you. I took the rope tied to the coffin and pulled it and Quin down to where the horse still grazed.

"We don't got to worry about them attacking out here in the open," I said. My reputation would prevent anything as direct as that. "But at night we're going to need some cover."

Quin thought about it for several long breaths. Then she said, "I think I know a place."

3

———

The sun set, and the wind picked up a fine ash, blowing it through the air like a charcoal fog. Visibility dropped to a hundred meters, then fifty. Skeletal trees, burned long ago, scraped at the sky like the fingers of an old man grasping at the passage of time.

The ancient entrance to an abandoned mine sat below us, perched on the side of the mountains. A single gaping maw opened straight into the rock, surrounded by the remains of several brick outbuildings. In all, Quin's safe, defensible location was everything an old cowboy might have asked for—except for the grizzly ambling around out front.

Muffin was tied down where she could drink at a muddy mountain stream just up from the cave. She'd be fine there for the night, far enough from our location that the bounty hunters might not find her. I sat with Quin, looking down at the bear. It was a big old bastard, fur tipped with white over flesh riddled with scars.

"It's a good spot," I said.

Quin chewed her lower lip like it was a lump of over-cured jerky.

"Well," I said, "I think we can make this work."

Her expression darkened but she said nothing. She'd led us to that spot without any hesitation, but never mentioned any bear. Either the bear was new or she'd forgotten about it. The moon sat fat up in the sky, and there we were with nowhere safe to rest.

"We can't kill that bear," she finally said.

"I'm not saying we should."

"There's a spot back in the mine that the bear can't get in. It's too big."

"You sure about that?"

Quin swallowed hard. No, then.

"There's two bounty hunters after us, Quin. Sunset is a mean lady with a flare for destruction. She prefers to bring in bounties alive, so they squirm, and she loves the hunt almost as much as victory. I've never met a more competent bounty hunter."

"We used to come down here all the time. There never was so much as squirrels back then."

"Casket Jones is worse," I said. "Mean as hell."

"I'm still not letting you kill the bear."

I furrowed my brow. "Is that what you think I'm fixin' to do?"

She gave a nod.

"Pay attention, kid."

I picked my way down the slope, pulling the coffin behind me and approaching upwind. No need to alert the bear to my presence if it could be helped. Once I was close, I kept the outbuildings between me and the beast, sneaking as best a man can sneak with cowboy boots and a bad back.

The closest building stood on a concrete foundation, but its stick frame had long since collapsed under the weight of years. I hunkered down behind the building, waiting while my heart stopped stammering. The bear was only fifty meters away, and a peek around the corner of the building told me it wasn't moving anymore. It curled in a ball at the foot of a cliff and lay there like a giant hairball.

I waved Quin forward, and after a brief hesitation, she came.

The second building was in much better shape but wasn't directly downwind of the bear. A roof would be nice to help conceal us if the hunters did an overhead scan. I edged around the broken building and made my way closer to the cave. Quin followed, quieter than I'd ever been, even in my army days. We reached the building and carefully moved the coffin through the open door. It was dark inside and stank of rat feces. Something scurried around in the dark, but when I lowered the coffin to the floor, nothing complained.

"Is this your plan?" Quin whispered. "Hide in a building?"

"One more thing," I said.

The corner of that building was only twenty meters from the mine entrance, and therefore twenty meters from the bear. From that close, I got a good look at its scarred face and the gray hairs around its muzzle. That old bastard had survived some tough days. To tell the truth, it gave me a sense of solidarity.

I slid off my boots, sure that they'd give me away if I moved so close to the bear. Tucking them under my armpit, I crept forward to the cave. Every step triggered a panicked pounding of my heart as every instinct in my body said to flee. Ten meters, then five. I could hear the bear's rasping breath as it inhaled the ashy air. It shifted, the casual shrug of its muscles changing the very air around it.

At the cave, I set my boots down where they'd be visible from the sky. Next to that, I set my hat on a rock. Finally, I took my cube, powered it up, and set it next to my hat.

Then I made my way back to the little building. When I was halfway there, the bear shifted. I felt its massive bulk through the soles of my feet, and for one long held breath, I was certain it had seen me. It stood on hind legs, towering over the ruined buildings around it. Then it dropped to all fours, the earth thundering under its feet. It moved lazily into the cave, taking a moment to sniff at the hat and boots before disappearing into the dark.

Back in the building, I waited until my heart slowed before whispering to Quin, "We'll keep an eye out. They'll think we're staying in the cave, and if we're quick we can pin them between us and the bear."

We didn't need to wait long.

Sunset descended on a yellow skidder, her thick, loping anti-grav near silent against the howl of the ashen wind. It had a sidecar and two mounted cannons. She was a big woman with dark skin, her face scarred and her knuckles calloused. She wore golden aviators and a red cowboy hat that matched her long red leather jacket. She looked like a joke of a bounty hunter, like what the fantasies about the job might have made up for entertainment videos. Unfortunately, she was as real as it got and a whole lot meaner.

Above, through the hazy sky, I spotted three smaller flyers, no doubt her team of thugs. I drew my pistol, a massive .50 caliber derived from the Desert Eagle. It didn't carry the Red Number Five that could punch through any armor, but a hit from this pistol would give even that bear second thoughts. I motioned for Quin to stay put, but she already had her shotgun out.

Sunset's bike touched down and she hopped off. No sooner had she left it, than she backed up against the cliff wall and touched a computer on her wrist. The motorcycle lifted and swung around, shining a flashlight straight down the tunnel entrance. So much for hoping they'd try to sneak up.

The three other flyers descended, one opposite Sunset outside the cave, one at the other building, and one not three meters from where I hid. The man on that bike, a reedy guy with greasy hair, peered into the darkness of our building. Since when did Sunset run with a crew?

Sunset broke the heavy silence. "J.D., get your ass out here!"

My heart pounded in my chest. The reedy guy turned to watch the cave entrance; his revolver already drawn.

Sunset hazarded a peek into the cave, but only for a fraction of a second. "I've been chasing that bounty long as you have, old man. Come on out here and let's negotiate."

I knew a trap when I smelled one. Sunset wasn't the negotiating type.

The guy close to me took a step toward the building. His counterpart at the broken-down building was already inside, making a thorough check of the location. I could expect the same soon.

But I wasn't going to wait for it. In one quick move, I stepped out, grabbed the guy's head in my giant left hand, and yanked him toward us. Quin leveled her shotgun at him, but I waved her off.

With my hand almost crushing the guy's head, he didn't dare shout. I disarmed him and slid his weapon aside. Our eyes met, and I winked, putting a finger to my lips. He understood the agreement. Stay shut and you'll live. I slipped an e-cuff from my pocket and attached it behind his left ear where a glint of metal shone. It'd shut down every mechanical system in his body just to prevent him from getting too unruly. It was a tech I'd kept from my sheriff days and fairly handy in the bounty hunting business.

"Keep this guy quiet," I whispered to Quin. "Don't shoot unless you have to."

She nodded and leveled her shotgun at the man's chest. When he didn't protest, I let go of his skull. When he still didn't protest, I moved back to the door.

Sunset and her thug were gone. Disappeared into the bear's cave, probably.

That left the one guy in the other building. I made my way across the rocky landscape, sharp stones digging into the bottoms of my feet. If I could sneak up on him—if I could be quick—maybe I could take him down without making a sound. It'd make the business with Sunset and her other goon that much easier.

The wind picked up the ashy haze, swirling it around as I padded across the open space between buildings. My heart hammered like a drum, and adrenaline made my mouth dry. Once in place, I hazarded a peek over a short wall. The guy was there, heavyset and wearing leather like it was body armor. It might have been. I hunkered down behind the wall and listened. When he took a few steps closer, I pounced, hoping to knock him out with one hard blow. Clean and quiet.

It didn't go that way.

My metal left arm swung for his head, blocked by a lightning quick flash of his own metal arm. Shit. I should have figured on augments.

He gave out a shout and unleashed a flurry of punches with his other fist, his metal arm still holding mine. I twisted, using my mass to shift his angle of attack. Instead of falling back, he pressed his advantage by moving with me and landing two painfully vicious blows to my skull.

I braced and tried to move him again, but without boots my feet couldn't get traction. Instead, I retreated, getting my poor head as far away from his fists as I could.

With the extra distance, he had time to draw his weapon. He let go of my arm, but by then he had his revolver out and pointed at my chest.

"Now hold still," he said. "Sunset's not here for you."

A long moment passed with us both frozen. The look in his eyes said he didn't want to shoot. The look in mine probably said I didn't want to get shot. Didn't mean I'd back down. The man's hand shook, not enough to vary his shot but enough for me to sense his hesitation. Instinct kicked in whenever something like this crept into my life. I recognized him.

"You've been in my jail," I said, my voice resonating deep with authority. "Lot of folks know me by reputation, but you're one I handled straight up."

The thug said nothing.

I forced a relaxed posture. "Yeah, I remember you. Mean Johnny Ratchet, right? You got caught up in an ugly gang for a while. Cinco Armas, if I recall. One of Court's boys. Served a little time behind bars before you left for the city. How did Austin treat you, by the way?"

"I did my time." The barrel of his pistol wavered a little more. Sweat beaded on Mean Johnny's brow.

"Sure, sure," I said. "You did. Now you've got a better gang. One that's not robbing banks. They're not above robbing the occasional bounty hunter, but what's that matter to the law? Nothing but honor keeps us hunters in line, isn't that right?"

A vein in his neck twitched. "Hunting sure as shit beats working for Goodwin."

I remembered the first time I met Chester Goodwin. He was a weasel and a fool and now head of the corrupt and powerful Goodwin Dairy. He'd inherited the whole company from his equally corrupt father. Chester Goodwin had leveraged that behemoth of a corporation into a bully powerful enough to shove around all of Texas. "You know that asshole?"

Johnny took a step back. "I could shoot you."

I took a step forward. "You could. Or you disappear into those woods and leave Sunset to fend for herself. You know she'd do the same for you. Honor don't mean nothing to someone like her, Johnny. Let me take care of things here."

His breathing quickened. Tension rolled through his jaw like a taut wire. "Sheriff," he said.

"I ain't a sheriff no more."

"You ruined my life when I was a kid. You sent me up when

you didn't need to." He raised the gun again, pointing straight at my face. "You fucking killed me."

I tried to keep my voice as calm as I could. "You don't look dead."

"I fucking am!"

The bear roared.

There are many kinds of roars. Some are little more than large yawns. Animals in the wild communicate with noise, and the raw emotion they put into their roars speak volumes, transcending all language. Some roars travel several kilometers, warning competitors to stay away. Other roars are exuberant and exciting. There are roars of pain, and of the wounded animal. Those are more like the screams of the dying or the piteous calls of the helpless or the defiance of the trapped.

And then there are roars of fury, murder, and death.

The roar that came out of that cave was the most frightening noise I'd ever heard. Johnny flinched, twisting to look in that direction.

I swung an open metal hand, slamming it into his gun hand. Bones cracked under the powerful blow, and the gun flew off into the dark.

Mean Johnny looked at me, the whites of his eyes showing his fright. I took hold of his metal arm and punched him hard in the head with my human fist. Pain shot down the length of my arm, like something tore right through it. Blood soaked my filthy bandage. His head snapped back, and I swung him down, slamming him hard onto the floor.

He stayed still.

Gunshots sounded from the cave. Flashes of white-hot phosphorous lit the inside of that gaping maw like lightning blazing across the sky.

I stalked across the broken terrain, hand hovering above my holstered pistol. When Sunset came out, I'd need to confront her fast.

It wasn't Sunset who flew from the cave. The thug tumbled across the rocks, a broken plaything for the massive monster. More gunshots flashed in the cave.

"Sunset!" I hollered. "Get your ass out of here!"

"J.D.?" Sunset's voice was a tight-wound spring. "Is that you?"

"Well, who the hell else did you think you ambushed?"

"Get me out of here, J.D." Another gunshot, as if it might be doing some good.

At the cave entrance, in the light of Sunset's hovering bike, I could see the situation Sunset had found herself. She'd backed herself into a corner, with the jutting walls of the cave forming a small alcove where the bear couldn't reach her. Quin had been right about the hiding spot. The air smelled of burned fur and seared flesh, but the angry bear didn't look terribly worse off. Apart from a spotting of blood-matted fur, it appeared to have endured the insults of bullets without much inconvenience. The sight almost made me laugh.

"Got yourself in a pickle," I said.

The bear let out a loud snort. It didn't look my way, and I wondered if it had trouble hearing. That would explain why it allowed Sunset and her thug to get so dangerously close before confronting them.

Sunset holstered her weapon. It wasn't doing her any good anyway. "Get me out of here, J.D. I was just going to talk."

"I had him listed as captured," I said. "Done all right the way it should."

"My employer wants him dead, and that's a separate bounty," Sunset said. "Francis Brown has it coming, and nobody knows that better than you."

She had that much right. I slipped on my boots and hat. Shrugged on my coat. "It's a damn shame you didn't give me a call first. I might have had a few words for you about that." With that, I turned to leave.

"J.D.!" Sunset yelled. "Get your ass back here and move this bear!"

"He'll move," I said, not bothering to turn back. "When he's good and ready."

Sunset was still swearing up a storm when I found my way back to the building where Quin still held a shotgun to a man's chest. Without saying a word, I took the rope from the man's belt, hogtied him, and secured him to a slab of concrete with some rebar sticking out of it.

Quin watched me, jaw hanging loose. "Couldn't you have done that before?"

"Yup."

"Why didn't you?" Her eyes went to my bloody bandage.

"Well, then it wouldn't have kept you busy."

With that, we took the coffin with Francis Brown and made our way back up the mountain to pick up Muffin by the creek. There was more traveling to do, and not much of a good reason to stick around not doing it. We'd be damn fools to be anywhere nearby when Sunset finally found her way out of the cave. Chances were, we were damn fools anyway.

4

____

We walked down the middle of a wide road, the moon a silver smudge across the still-hazy sky. The ashen wind let us be, only returning for the occasional tug at our backs. Even in the relatively bright moonlight from the clearing sky, it was too much of a risk to walk Muffin through the uneven trails. The road might be harder on the old horse's knees, but it was preferable to twisting an ankle on the uneven earth of the burned forest. Behind her, Francis's coffin drifted in silence like a big white ghost.

I flexed my right hand, which still ached something fierce after slugging Johnny. Rebandaging it had hurt like hell, and the wound hadn't closed up as nicely as I would have liked. We'd walked hours without speaking, and I'd just started to kindle some hope that it could stay that way.

"Won't they come after us?"

I considered it. "I give it about fifty-fifty."

"You could have killed them. They attacked us."

"They did."

"So, if you'd killed them, we'd be safe right about now."

I shook my head. "You weren't so eager to kill that bear."

"That's different. The bear wouldn't track us down and knife us in our sleep."

"Fifty-fifty ain't bad odds."

Quin looked at me, a horrified expression on her face. "How are you even so old?"

I took out a cigarette, stuck it between my lips, and lit it. "Rugged charm."

She made a disgusted noise.

"Look, kid, I made a promise a long time ago. Said I wouldn't kill anyone if I could help it. Promises are important."

"Important enough to get the both of us killed?"

"A fair bit more important than that." I turned to regard her. "A person's honor is bigger than them. It's the thing that holds everything together, even when the law breaks down way out here in the wild. Give that up and you're as good as dead anyway."

After that, she didn't talk for a long while.

Truth was, fifty-fifty was probably generous, and it made me about as nervous as I was like to get. We needed refuge, and the nearest I could figure we'd find it was a town called Candlestick Crossing. Crossing wasn't the kind of place I'd lightly visit, and sure as hell not someplace I'd bring a kid. It was built into the wreck of a dead nuclear weapons factory—dead for lack of fuel, even if the ancient atom-smashing tech still lay in pristine ruins around the town. If there was a place outlaws feared to go more than a law-abiding town, it was Crossing, where the law was nothing more than gunmetal, knife blades, and raw muscle. A person who could survive that place could survive anywhere in the Texas wasteland.

Crossing would be better than the open road, but not by much. We could find transport there if I was able to avoid running into anyone who knew me. It was a tossup whether I had more enemies as a former sheriff or as a current asshole, but there were plenty out there either way.

We had thousands of kilometers to travel to deliver Francis, and it wasn't likely Muffin could do all that distance on the run. Even the fifty kilometers to Crossing was going to be a hell of a walk for her. She'd started nipping at my coat whenever I gave her a chance.

The land grew flat as the sky shifted grays in preparation for sunrise. Around us, the ashen forests gave way to scorched salt flats and twisted cacti. These lands had long ago been blasted clean by the ravages of mankind and the fury of the volcano. That they had anything alive at all was a miracle. That we thought we could cross it was damn near idiocy, but we didn't have much choice.

At the foot of the hills we found another creek, and I ate some dried meat while Muffin drank. Quin opened her own pack and ate a protein bar, tucking the wrapper away safely when she finished.

I lay down to rest my weary bones next to the creek. All at once, the weight of the previous day's events settled on my chest. I'd caught Francis William Brown: scourge of the Texas wastes, bane of the free and the strong. I'd sought him for years after the events of Swallow Hill. Times had been hard, and even in the worst of it I'd kept that kid in the back of my mind. He was a specter of my failure walking always one step ahead.

Now, he was caught, and I didn't know what to do with my life. For a time, I watched as Quin brushed Muffin down. She had a way with the horse, like nobody I'd ever met. Could be that she was just a kid looking to escape the poisonous pall of her small hometown. She'd need someone to help her get started if she wanted anything like a chance out in the world. No reason that someone couldn't be me.

I needed to suss out her motivation. What was she running from? What did she want from the world? Why didn't she leave long ago?

Later. My eyes were so damn heavy. I caught myself drifting

off several times, despite the rocks digging into the small of my back. All that could wait until after a ten-minute nap. Maybe twenty.

When I woke, the sun sat high in the sky. I blinked against the light and moaned.

"Morning," Quin said, stretching.

I swore. "How long was I out."

She shrugged. "Long enough."

Muffin stood a short distance away, still looking a little annoyed. No surprise, since the grazing wasn't much more than a few scrubby grasses and a short shrub that she'd mowed clean of its leaves.

We packed up our things, readied Francis's box, and left. I rode Muffin again, and Quin took her spot on the coffin.

"When we get to Crossing, you keep your mouth shut," I said to Quin. "Don't talk to anyone who hasn't talked to you."

"Crossing? Like, as in Candlestick Crossing? The outlaw town?"

"It's not an outlaw town," I said. "It just happens to have a large outlaw population."

"And no laws." Quin grinned.

"It has laws," I said. "It's just that they aren't written down and they're enforced at random by anyone who happens to think you look funny."

Quin's grin didn't fade.

I put my hand on her shoulder. "You look funny, Quin. Keep your mouth shut so nobody notices."

Candlestick Crossing appeared like a dark smudge across the horizon. There at the edge of town stood the Candle—a fat rocket standing sentinel—blazing with the reflected light of the bright sun. We followed a set of train tracks for the last few kilometers, keeping a close eye on the skies above for any trouble. There was plenty, but none of it came for us. Skidders rocketed in and out of town on a regular basis, with flying cars gracing the clear day less frequently. Some ran in gangs. Most were solitary.

Closer, a train at the Candlestick Crossing station came into view. The sleek shining thing with sloped aerodynamic lines and a blue cast to its chrome exterior stuck out like a ray of sunlight on an overcast day. The top-of-the-line locomotive stood a stark contrast to the town, which was composed of a ramshackle collection of old ruined buildings and new ruined buildings. Only six dozen structures made up the town proper, with a couple dozen more dotting the neighboring hills. There were ranches farther out, and small farms to help feed the community. Tough living for honest folk, but anyone willing to defend their land could do well near Crossing. A lot of money, legitimate or otherwise, poured through the little community.

Quin gaped at it all, wide-eyed.

"Shut your mouth," I said under my breath.

Quin shut it.

"I'll find us a place to stay."

There were only two options of places to stay the night in Crossing. One of them was bleeding out in the ditch, and the other wasn't a whole hell of a lot better. It stood two stories tall, the recovered concrete structure of what used to be an old motel. The clerk at the counter gave us a key in exchange for a few stars but didn't bother to look me in the eye as he pocketed the tarnished coins. Best not to get attached. The room we had was ground floor, so I shoved the coffin inside, dropping it next to the bed.

Quin stood and stared at the mess of a room in stunned silence. The beds weren't made, and there was a dark stain on the wall behind it. There was a bathroom with something that looked like it might have once been indoor plumbing. It didn't smell like it worked. The hot summer heat amplified all the unpleasantness of the place, ratcheting the stink up three or four notches until it hardly even registered on the scale. It would be an unpleasant place to sleep, but not the worst accommodations I'd ever been in.

"Still sure you want to get out and see the world, kid?" I asked as I tied Muffin up out front. The clerk at the desk had sold me some oats, and the horse was finally getting the decent meal she needed.

Quin got a far-off look for a second. "Yeah," she said finally. "Yeah, I think so."

"Good. Let's lock old Francis down here and go get a bite."

"We're leaving him?"

I gestured to a little tavern across the street. "Anything funny happens, we'll be able to see it from over there."

She chewed her lower lip. "This is a town of criminals."

The coffin flashed once as I engaged the alarms. My glow cube flashed in sequence in my hand. "State of the art," I said.

Quin eyed the cube. I'd owned the device for more years than I could count, and it still worked as well as it always had: not very well.

"It's unhackable," I said.

"It's ancient."

"Well, the coffin's got state-of-the-art defenses. Anyone messing with it is going to alert us fast enough."

The tavern was the newest building on this side of town. By the time we moseyed through the front door, the sun had gone down again, and the front of the place was lit with flickering lamps. Inside, the place smelled of stale cigars and fresh whiskey. I ordered up one of each for the both of us, but Quin refused the cigar. We sat at a table where I could have my back to the wall and a view of the door to our hotel room.

Hours passed, and after a plate of ribs each, Quin and I settled in for an evening of drinks. The place filled up with rough sorts, and with the low murmur of casual discontent the place almost reminded me of home.

Outside, a group of three men in black loitered with a look

on their faces that might have kept me employed in my sheriff days. They had trouble hanging about them, but they didn't wander close to our motel.

"What's so bad back home?" I asked. "You running from something?"

Quin took a sip of her whiskey, winced, and set it down. "Not exactly," she said.

I downed my whiskey in one big gulp. It burned its way down, but I knew it wasn't going to have much effect. I'd fought an alcohol problem since the war, and the worst part of it was that the nanomachines in my blood wouldn't let me get properly intoxicated. Still, the burn of the drink did something to soothe my raw nerves. We had a long road ahead, and it wasn't going to do me much good burning out early.

"Hey," I said to the barkeep when I ordered another whiskey. "How long is that train in for?"

"Just got in town," the man said. "They're loading it up tomorrow, and it probably leaves quick after that."

Standing at the bar, I took a good look at Quin. It hadn't bothered me much bringing her with. Nobody had come after her, and she was old enough to make decisions on her own. I wondered how far she'd ever traveled from her wasteland town. Had this really been her first trip out of the mountains? A kid at a certain age is bound to wander some. Having her along with me meant I could protect her from the worst of it, but it sure as hell wasn't going to be a vacation.

As if to illustrate the point, the three men in black detached from their leaning post to surround a woman in the street. They started with a false charm, standing too close, casually surrounding her. The woman stood in a carmine blue suit, loose fitting and sleek all at once. She didn't slow for the men until one of them stood in her path. She stopped.

"Should we do something?" Quin asked as I sat back down.

"There's a code 'round these parts. If you can't handle your own business, you're as good as dead." It felt wrong saying it, as if I might be admitting that the law was always worthless. "If we went out and helped, we'd be causing a load of trouble."

The three men closed their circle around the woman, laughing as if it were all a casual joke. She still didn't look any of them in the eye.

"But there are three of them," Quin said. "And they're big."

I chuckled. "You know better than most that big don't win fights."

"That's football."

"Football's just another battlefield."

The woman finally looked up at the leader's face. She plucked the toothpick out of his mouth and flicked it into the air.

"Anyway," I said, "she doesn't need our help."

The woman moved like a snapped spring. In a sequence too fast to follow, she bloodied the two men behind her with elbows, broke an arm of the fella in front of her, drew two pistols, fired one shot each into both feet of each man, holstered her twin pistols, and smoothed her suit as if it might show a wrinkle after so much movement. It didn't. She still looked as perfect as she'd been the last time I'd seen her.

I left the bar with arms wide open. "Contrisha Chin," I said. "Who'd have thought I'd run into you out here?"

Trish had been sheriff of Dead Oak when I'd last left town half a decade ago. By all accounts she'd been a good sheriff, fair and strong. Still was, as far as I knew. She wore a star on her blue suit, and even though her skin hadn't aged one minute since I'd left, her eyes looked at me with the kind of wise wisdom only hard years can bring.

"J.D." She shook my hand, then pulled me into an embrace. "It's been tough out there, old man."

"I know," I said. "I know."

She pulled away, smoothed her suit again, and looked at Quin. "Where's Francis?"

I folded my arms. "He's safe, but I was delivering him to Dead Oak for you."

Gingerly stepping around one of the men still writhing in pain on the street, Quin stood by my side. She jutted her chin out defiantly.

I stepped over one of the men in the direction of the hotel. If she wanted to do the exchange early, then I'd do it early. "This way," I said.

Trish said, "I figured I'd better fly all the way up here for the pickup."

That interested me. Normally, I kept my tech profile low so I wouldn't make an easy score, but she'd tracked me just fine. I rode a horse and rarely communicated via wireless technology. I hadn't sent any signals since I'd come to town, and if Trish was able to find me so easily, then I probably had to worry about someone else finding me as well. The thought of it made me itch.

"Lot about this doesn't smell right," I said. "How did you find me?"

Quin said in a quiet voice, "J.D.?"

Trish sized me up with a dull look. "You really want me getting into technical details?"

I sure as hell didn't. "Sunset hit us as we came down the forest."

Trish shook her head. "I'm not worried about Sunset."

"No, you're probably not."

Quin tugged my sleeve. "Hey."

"What?" I failed to keep the annoyance from my voice.

"Your pocket's glowing."

Sure enough, the glow cube in my front pocket shook like a frightened rabbit. It took me a long several seconds to figure out what it meant. The coffin's alerts were triggered. Someone was near the coffin.

It went black. I turned to the door to our hotel room, not ten meters away. That room hadn't left our sight since we'd stuffed Francis's coffin in it. Now it stood there oozing dread right into the left ventricle of my stone cold heart. I'd trusted technology. Depended on the state-of-the-art fancy coffin to do my work when I should have stayed put.

Quin and Trish watched me as I took my first step toward that door. I should have killed that bastard when I had the chance. If any damn fool deserved a knife in the gut it was Francis William Brown. Another step. The air moved like molasses as the world came crashing down around me. How could anyone have stolen the coffin? No way they went out the door. The only door.

I unlocked the door and pushed it open real slow.

The back wall of the room was a gaping hole, cut nice and clean in a smooth rectangle.

The coffin, of goddamn course, was gone.

5

———

"Well, there it is then," I said, sitting on the corner of the shabby bed so my legs wouldn't give out under me. "Had my chance. Might be another decade before I get another."

Trish drew one of her pistols and moved to the gaping hole in the back of the room. After peering out for a second, then checking the angles, she disappeared into a narrow alley.

The air tasted of rot. "It was a damn fine chance too. Should have put a bullet in the kid when I had a chance." I looked up at Quin. "Why the hell didn't I?"

She looked more scared of me than she had been of Sunset's goons. What did I look like to her at that moment? "We'll get him back."

I shook my head. "How's that going to go down? Whoever took the coffin wasn't just collecting souvenirs. They came here for him and they've probably already left town."

Trish came in through the front door. "Not likely," she said. "I'm watching traffic and nothing big enough to haul that coffin has left. Soon as it does, I'll be right after it."

"They could have set him free."

"Well, then they set him free. Assume they didn't."

The room spun around me, and not from the trace effects of the alcohol. There'd been a sense of freedom when I'd finally captured Francis Brown. Some tensed muscle in me had finally relaxed and now that it tried flexing again, it wouldn't work. I was broken.

"There's nothing we can do," I said. "No hints who took him. No way to stop him from leaving town."

Trish looked at me like I was a dying mutt.

"We got one clue," Quin said.

It took several seconds for the comment to sink in through my skull. When it did, all I said was, "What?"

Quin pointed at a spot behind me on the bed, among the disheveled blankets. On one particularly chaotic tangle of cloth sat a single metallic rectangle the size of a playing card. When I saw it, my heart started pounding like it was making up for lost time. I picked up the card, making a conscious effort to steady my hand. The steel card carried a pattern in its brushed surface —a five of spades with a single phrase printed along the bottom.

Come alone.

Shit.

"What is it?" Quin asked.

"A promise." I slipped the card into my coat pocket. "One I made a good long while ago." I met Trish's eyes until I was sure she read my meaning in it. She'd have to get Quin out of town if I didn't come back. "I need to go have a conversation."

"With who?" Trish said.

I showed her the five of spades. "I think you know."

Trish put a hand on my shoulder, but it didn't make me feel one bit better. I tipped my hat to Quin, brushed the nonexistent dust off my coat, and ventured out into the now-darkened streets. Somewhere in the distance, a single gunshot rang out. The streets of the tiny dirt ball of a town got busier as darkness swallowed the sky. Men carousing, women whooping in exultation in a raw celebration of a life full to the brim with excitement and adventure. These people were alive in a way I'd rarely ever been. It made me uncomfortable.

I rounded the corner and not ten meters away stood Sunset, walking toward me with thugs in tow. My poor heart set to hammering at the inside of my ribcage. Another gunshot rang out in the distance. One more much closer.

Sunset's expression was unreadable. Her thugs eyed me like a coyote eyes a wolf—pure spite mixed with a touch of hunger—but the woman in the bright red hat didn't show anything at all. As I approached each step of my boot snapped against the gravel like the sound of my own doomsday clock. She watched me approach, here cold calculating eyes picking me out in the light from nearby lamps.

She tipped her hat, a twinkle of amusement finally coming to her eye. I tipped back, and moved on my way.

The adrenaline got my mind racing—snapped me out of the funk I'd been in since losing Francis. Hell, I'd been in a funk since capturing him. Sunset wasn't the one who stole him out from under me, so that left Casket Jones as the main suspect. Him, or somebody working directly with Francis. Someone who was paid to set the man free.

But how had they tracked me so fast? How did they know exactly where to find the coffin?

Those questions would have to wait. I drew the metal card from my pocket and held it in front of the establishment now in front of me.

The Cinco Pala was a wart of a fortress on the ass end of the little town. The big black lump of a building jutted from the yellow rock with deep violet lights illuminating the surrounding buildings. It was a nightclub, emerging from the earth the way criminal gangs emerge from an otherwise peaceful populations—both unwanted and adored.

Crossing wasn't a peaceful population, and nobody around

disdained the lump of a building glowing violet and thundering with bass so deep it rattled the very foundation of the town. Clusters of patrons lingered in the streets outside, eyeing newcomers like me. There were others who clearly didn't belong—green gunslingers out to make their name in the world. Others had an air of official authority, as if they might be the thugs policing the area, but what crimes they sought, anyone might guess. As I walked up to the Cinco Pala, two fights broke out and one of them ended in a brutal death.

Head down, I passed through the gate into a large entryway. Along one wall, a counter sat where folks checked their weapons. Grudgingly, I set my guns and knives on the table. No use trying to sneak anything in. The scan I passed through after that would find anything I was stupid enough to hide.

Inside, I descended some steps into the pulsing five-chambered heart of an adrenaline junkie. Five stages sat at the ends of five large halls, their various double-dubbed mixes wrecking at the center, mashing into an arrhythmic mess of noise and color. The deep-violet lights outside pulsed here, reacting to the chaotic waves of music that exploded through the halls and destroyed my senses. I headed left, where the long hall had a slightly lighter shade of violet and not so many patrons pressing in the crowd.

Soon as I'd stepped to that side, the music ordered itself, acoustics filtering the noise into one singular sound—a guitar twang accompanied by a thundering drumbeat. In this chamber, the skeletal remains of once-productive factory equipment lined the walls. Still-shining equipment flashed in the laser display mounted atop the open stage. People here mingled about standing tables, bottles of beer the focus of long, hard stares. I moseyed up to the bar and ordered one for myself.

The beer was good—light and hoppy. The smooth cold of it did my nerves little good as I waited, sure that it wouldn't be long.

It wasn't.

"A girl could almost think you were avoiding her," said an androgynous voice behind me.

"Nice place you have here, Court," I said without turning.

"It's this results of good, honest work, Sheriff. You should try it sometime." Court was the head of the largest gang in the region, maybe in all of Texas. Cinco Armas had its grubby fingers in every pie outside of Austin and rumor held that it even held some influence inside the city.

I turned to give her a good look. Court was tall and slender, with four arms and a smile that hinted of secrets and malice. When she moved, it was with a grace and confidence that befitted the wealthy youth, and heads turned as she glided across the floor. Everything she wore glinted with hidden tech, and I had no doubt that most of it was a weapon of some sort.

"I want that coffin back," I said.

"Not the man inside?"

I took a swig of my beer. "Figured you already killed him." Francis's grasp of technology was more a threat to her and her organization than anything else. The terrible things he'd do to Austin, if given the chance, would hit Cinco Armas like a runaway freighter.

Court leaned close to me, her lips brushing against my ear. "It would be a shame to kill such a clever man."

"So that wasn't your bounty out on his head?"

"Do you think we couldn't handle such things in house?"

I fought the urge to shy away. The woman oozed danger. "Why did you take him, if not to finish him off?"

"You owe me a favor."

"I was hoping you forgot." I looked up when one of her four hands slowly raked its razor-sharp nails across my arm. "Fine, so you took Brown as payment. We're even."

She shook her head. "I took Brown to pay another debt, and

it's paid. That's how this works, J.D. That's how honor keeps us alive."

I washed away the bitter taste in my mouth with a swig of beer. It was all I could do to keep myself from debating the merits of her twisted version of honor. "What do you want then?"

"Promise not to kill Francis Brown."

The bottle slipped from my fingers, and in trying to catch it, I crushed it with my left hand. Beer and glass sprayed between the fingers of my metal hand. "No way I'm ever promising that."

A moment passed as she sized me up. "Fine," she said, "then let's talk about a sheriff friend of yours."

"You know I won't kill for you."

She pressed a hand to her chest in mock surprise. "Kill? Sheriff, you always think of the simplest solutions. No, it doesn't need to be murder, unless that's what you want. All I need is Sheriff Chin out of my business for a few days."

Trish was too damn smart to fall for any trick I'd send her way. Court's favor—earned when I was once too damn desperate—had been an axe hanging over my head for too long. This was a damn tempting offer. If I kept Trish close and brought her into my confidence, maybe I could keep her from whatever Court was trying. Maybe this would keep her safe, since Court wouldn't need to send a real killer.

But at what cost? If Trish fought against something Court was doing, then it must be something bad. No good could come from interfering. Trish didn't much like me in the first place. What would she say if she found out I'd ruined her one chance to take Cinco Armas down a notch?

Then again, I needed her help if I was going to have any chance at tracking down Francis. With her at my side, I could solve both our problems, and do the honorable thing in keeping my promise to Court.

"What makes you think I'll follow through?" I finally asked.

Her smile was a knife-edge. "You're a man of honor, Mr. Crow. You don't have a choice."

"Where's Francis?" I asked.

Court closed her eyes for a second. "They're loading him up on the train," she said.

"You have a deal," I said, "if you can get me on that train."

She took a step back and held my gaze for the space of several long breaths. "Automated security in the town or on the train won't bother you one bit, dear, but I can't do anything about his men once you're aboard."

"Whose men?"

She barked out a laugh as she turned to leave. It was a sharp, graceless thing, and hearing it from her shocked me. "It's the only man uglier than you, J.D. Crow, and the only man I know who holds more of a grudge." With that she disappeared into the pulsing noise of the Cinco Pala.

Shit. It was just who I feared. Francis had been taken by Casket Jones.

6

―――――

"Casket Jones is the meanest of the meanest," I said to Quin as we watched the moonlight bounce off the shining skin of the dormant bullet train. "Rumor has it, he came by his name when he got shot up one time. They were so sure he was dead that they scooped him into his casket."

"He wasn't dead, though," Trish said. "His experimental biomods give him something like fast healing. Far better than nanomachines."

A tall man, slender and long like someone stretched him out, stood atop the train: Casket Jones. A hat sat low over a tumor-ridden face, and his left arm was all lumpy like a mess of bee stings. His black button-down shirt blew in the breeze like it was hanging on a scarecrow. An icy maliciousness lurked deep in his dark eyes.

"He was shot a hundred times, they said." I hunkered back deeper into the shadow. "Maybe two hundred, depending on who you ask. He was a pincushion, and nobody but nobody could have survived that day. They said he was shot straight through the heart."

With a wave of a hand, Casket Jones signaled to his allies on the ground. They dragged Francis's coffin onto the train, loading it onto one of the cargo cars near the middle of the train.

Quin looked skeptical. "Casket Jones survived a hundred bullet wounds?"

"Maybe two hundred," Trish said. "The man was never quite right after that day. Something broke in his head."

Quin swallowed like there was something caught in her throat. On the train, Jones let out a whistle to signal to his men and waved them along.

"What did you ride into town?" I asked Trish.

"Nothing that'll keep up with that," she said, indicating the train. "But we know where that train's headed."

"Where?"

"Straight to the checkpoint in Dead Oak. Then Austin?"

"Why Dead Oak?"

"Nothing gets into Austin these days without a check in Dead Oak first. Chester Goodwin even comes out for the important shipments."

"Weapons?"

"All kinds of tech. We can catch up to them when they stop there."

I spat. "I'm not leaving without Francis."

"I'm not asking you to."

"We get on that train or we lose him. Simple as that."

Trish's shoulders tensed. "That's suicide, J.D. We don't have a plan and he could have a dozen guys on that train."

"Got any better ideas?"

Trish whispered, "Just because you only have bad ideas doesn't mean you have to follow through with them."

"It's always worked out in the past."

Trish put a hand on my shoulder. "I'll handle this, J.D. This is the kind of thing the law is for, remember? We can catch him on inspection."

I shook my head. "No laws being broken here, Sheriff. It's bounty hunter code, but that's a far spit from the law."

Casket Jones looked our direction, to where we hid in the shadows of an empty storefront. A hint of a smirk slithered across his face.

"I gotta get in there," I said. I checked my weapon at my hip, but my hand still ached something fierce from the punch I'd landed on Sunset's metal-skulled goon. The cut from Francis's claws still seeped, and my bandage was caked in red dust.

"It's leaving soon," Quin said. "We should all get on."

"No," both Trish and I said simultaneously.

Quin frowned. She likely didn't appreciate being left behind, but it couldn't be helped. I had some business to take care of. Then again, I couldn't exactly leave her alone.

"I'll sneak on, grab the coffin, and leave," I said. Saying it didn't make it sound any more plausible. "Might need to throw a few punches." Remembering Court's request, I touched Trish's arm. "Trish," I said, using my most sincere voice. "I need you to stick with the kid. Stay out of this town's business for a few days."

"This town's business is *my* business, J.D."

"I need you to back off."

"There's a deal going down—maybe already happened." She peered at the train. "I'm close. This is a major weapons deal, and I almost have them. You think I can just back off?"

"You're a stronger person than I ever was."

Her eyes searched mine for answers, and when I didn't give any, she did me the favor of not asking. All she said was, "Stronger, but maybe not more stubborn."

"Quin won't be safe if you press things right now. Stay low till I get back." Asking it of her hurt like a knife in my gut.

Trish said, "You're right, the law doesn't get much traction here. This is bounty hunter business." She said it like the words tasted like cow chips. "I'll wait till you come back."

Casket Jones walked down the length of the train away from us, so I used the opportunity to stroll all casual-like to the far side of the train.

The bullet train was designed for speed and stability, and every external feature was smoothed over for better aerodynamics. It took several long seconds to find the door in the side of one car in the middle, but when I pressed it, the panel slid open for me. I tipped my hat forward and ducked inside. The door slid shut behind me.

I was in an empty cargo car, with bleach-white walls covered in a powdery grime. The back of the train had a single narrow window, revealing the long rails curving back through town and into the distance. My feet buzzed with the power humming in the depths of the train. It used antigrav to support its massive bulk, and those fields warmed up, even as I moved through the cars.

A sealed tunnel connected the cars, and I was still three away from where the other bounty hunter had taken that coffin. I flexed my hand. Still painful. The nanomachines in my blood could accelerate healing, but it still took time. It'd hurt like hell, but could still fire a weapon if I needed. Best not to try.

I entered the next car, which was a damn engineering experiment. The center of the space was dominated by a long steel barrel, with arms that reached out to bolt to the interior of the train. Three men worked, assembling pieces to the device. I tipped my hat to one of men as I squeezed past. These were the same men Trish had bludgeoned and shot the night before, and they looked well humbled for the abuse. One of them tipped his hat back, but the look in his eyes spoke bloody murder.

The narrow tunnel buzzed with a particularly rough rattle. The antigrav was wearing out there, but the slight twist in my belly told me it likely still functioned well enough. In the next car, I found more passengers, seated in rows. Ten men, all wearing black, same as the men in the previous car.

Like it was a uniform.

Behind me, the door between cars opened, and the three men followed me in.

I did my best to ignore them, powering forward until I reached the end of that car. Shouldering through, fast as I could, I muscled my way into the car where Francis's coffin sat next to a collection of cube storage.

The boy I'd hunted all those years and finally caught was now nothing but excess luggage. I eyed the button on the wall that would emergency decouple the cargo bay doors. They used a hard open so the thing could serve for emergency evacuation in case of impending high-speed collision. All I had to do was hit hard enough to bust the safety glass and I'd be able to run with the coffin.

"I think you'd best be stepping off the train," said a man in black with a scruffy beard. "This is your stop."

Now, a wise man might have stepped off that train. Sure as hell it hadn't gone as I'd expected. This wasn't a train geared out for passengers and cargo. Maybe it was the uniforms that the men wore or the rigid cube storage containers boxed around Francis's coffin. Perhaps some long-dead instinct had resurrected itself to nudge me in the direction of the lawman I once was. The thing was, something felt off about these folks and this train. Nothing I could tell you would point at what it was, but the wrongness compelled me to stupidity the way it had so many other times during my inexplicably long life.

"I'm here to see Jones," I said. "Casket Jones."

The man with the scruffy beard stepped around me to block the door to the next car. "Casket isn't seeing people right now," he said. "Come back later."

I stepped into the man's space. "Now, see, that's where I have a problem. This here train's fixin' to move, and I have business with Jones before it leaves."

He stood with his arms crossed, chest puffed up in a foolish attempt to look intimidating. His biceps rippled under his black shirt, and a muscle in his jaw twitched. A quick glance told me three others had entered the car, but none of them had drawn a weapon. Good. That meant things could stay civilized.

I smiled. It was my best smile, sincere enough to wrinkle the corners of my eyes. Maybe the charm of youth had long since left me, and the glow of innocence was a long lost sparkle in my eye, but when I meant no harm my smile could still win.

"Show him in," a voice said through a tinny speaker somewhere in the ceiling.

Scruffy's shoulders visibly relaxed. He nodded at one of the guys behind me, and the guy came up and unclipped my weapon holster. They took the whole belt, leaving me minus my two favorite weapons. Patting me down, they found my hunting knife, several old e-cuffs, and my little glow cube computer.

"I'm gonna want those back," I said.

The guy who took them left toward the rear car, and Scruffy motioned me forward, as if escorting a man of the highest honor.

We passed through two more cars on our way to see Casket Jones. The first was another passenger car, empty except for seven crates along one wall. They were weapon crates far as I could tell, and the air smelled of fresh gun oil.

In the next car, a fully stocked lab stood, its tables all bolted to the steel walls of the compartment. A man in a lab coat looked up as I entered, and I couldn't help but notice how his leg was shackled to the floor.

"Howdy," I said.

He shook like a leaf in a sandstorm. His eyes went to the equipment on one bench, and I'll be damned if it wasn't one of the most suspicious setups I'd ever seen. All the parts of makeshift bombs sat there in various states of assembly. Worse, right next to a rig of biological growth chambers sat the mother of all aerosol distributors. This fella was making something bad.

Damn bad, and by the look of the shackle on his leg, he wasn't doing it willingly.

"I'll come back and deal with you," I said.

The next car was one from the engine, and it was Casket Jones's own personal kingdom. There wasn't access farther forward, and everything in the train's workings was automated and computerized.

Casket's room had lush carpet, brass fixtures, and windows that shone like spotlights in the morning sun. Casket Jones sat on a small sofa along one wall, next to a mahogany desk that dominated half the room. He looked up at me, his mismatched eyes smiling at the amusement I'd brought him.

"J.D. Crow," he said, as his tumorous face struggled to smile. "You here to join the revolution?"

Before I could answer, the background noise changed, and the whole train bucked. We were moving.

7

"You took something that belongs to me," I said. My chances of getting off the train got worse with every jolt of acceleration. The humming floor buzzed in my boots.

"I think you have an antiquated understanding of ownership, my fellow hunter. Out here, possession's the boss of ownership." Casket Jones didn't rise from his lounging place on the sofa, but with a wave he dismissed Scruffy, who had followed me in. "You took Francis Brown, then I took him. It isn't really any more complicated than that."

My whole body tensed. He must have seen the anger working at my jaw. Long ago I'd believed I could bring justice to Texas. I'd thought there was some higher right and wrong that ruled how folks ought to act. Peace could exist in the world, and that when people held civilization close to their hearts they could exist in harmony with each other and the world around them. The ruins of Texas said otherwise. In my old age, I'd swallowed that poison cynicism same as everyone else, but I didn't much like it pointed out.

"You're telling me he's mine if I take him?"

Casket looked at me, eyes sparkling in the simulated gaslight in the brass wall fixtures. "I'd like your support, J.D. I'll give him to you if you join my crew."

"Keep your damn war."

He shook his head. "It's not mine to keep. It belongs to all of Texas. The city folk are winning, and legend tells that you're one of the best out there for fighting urban warfare."

"That was a long time ago."

He looked me up and down. It almost felt dirty the way he scanned the whole of me. "It's strategy we're interested in." He tapped his temple. "Brains win wars, you know. This train is going to be our big rallying cry, but if we don't play it right, we're not going to be able to capitalize on it."

I looked around at his cushy cabin. "Not much to capitalize on here. Just a train on its tracks, same as any other."

His face twisted into a shark-like smile. Several of his teeth had been replaced with wicked sharp chrome, and their razor edges dug into his flesh. With a groan that might have been pain and might have been pleasure, he stood. "You can't take Francis from me, J.D. If you want him, you're going to have to come with me. At least look at what we're doing here and we'll see if we can work something out."

War. I'd had my fill of war when I'd first stepped out onto the battlefield so many years ago. Jones wanted to drag me into a new war fought on the same damn lines for the same damn reasons. How much of this had Casket Jones planned? Was this why it'd been so easy to catch Francis? Was Jones behind crippling the man so I could easily take him? Was he responsible for leaking Francis's location so I could find him?

Down that road lay a whole pile of paranoia. Might as well have blamed the lukewarm oatmeal I had for breakfast on Casket Jones. All I knew was that the man's shark smile behind the tumorous mask of his face made a shiver run up my back.

Outside the window, the red rock blurred. Despite the steady feel of the floor, the train was already cruising fast enough to kill. No way could I leap to freedom, even if I could blast a way out. At this speed, I'd be so much grits across the rocky landscape.

A gun lay on Casket's desk. It was a long sleek thing made of red metal that shone in the morning sun like fresh blood. If I could get it, I'd stand a decent chance of fighting my way out, but that left me nowhere to run and a whole pile of men in black to fight.

Casket must have seen where my eyes were going. "Good," he said. "I'd hate to have you join without considering all your options." Again, the shark smile. "Consider this, though: Would I leave a loaded weapon on my desk? What if I left an empty weapon just to see if you'd go for it?"

"Only a damn fool fires a gun he didn't clean and load himself."

"Only a damn fool," he repeated mockingly. "Does that mean I should think you won't consider it? You've got a track record, you know. It's not the wise man who goes after Francis Brown, after all."

"But it's my brains you want for your war."

"Your face, really."

I clenched my fist so hard my knuckles cracked. The ache down deep in the joints still bothered me, but adrenaline washed out anything that might have stopped me from what I did next.

"There's no way out," Casket Jones said, all amusement dropped from his voice. "Help out the cause. Help *your* people, and you can have Francis back in his fancy coffin."

"Or else what?"

He shot a look at the window. The train ran atop the edge of a long canyon. "Or else my boys will help you leave right now. Alone."

The joints of my metal hand scraped as I clenched it into a fist.

Jones's eyes flicked to the hand. When people suspect I'm a threat they follow my guns and they look at my big metal hand. Those are the threats, as far as they can figure.

I sucker punched Casket as hard as I could with my human hand. The punch landed solid and something snapped inside my fist. Sharp, molten-lead pain ran all the way up my arm. Casket hollered and swore, stumbling back to the desk.

With a single step back, I tore the door straight off its hinges with my metal hand and threw it hard at Casket. It hit his red metal gun as he brought it up, sending the weapon flying from his crushed hand.

I ducked through the doorway, surprising Scruffy, who was busy harassing the scientist. With a big metal backhand, I sent him spinning to the floor. I grabbed the scientist's shackle and yanked it from the floor. Without another look at him, I tore off the door to the next car and held it behind me as a shield.

"You're a dead man, J.D.," Casket shouted. He fired twice, but he was a garbage shot with his left hand. Both shots glanced off the door. The gun *was* loaded.

The scientist cowered in the corner, eyes like bull's-eyes.

"What's your name?" I said.

"Reginald."

With a furious sweep of the metal arm I crushed as much lab equipment as I could manage. "Come on, then, Reggie. Let's get out of here."

He darted through the door, my cover blocking two more shots from Casket's fancy gun. No—not a fancy gun. It was a regular gun made to look fancy. Somehow that seemed appropriate. Whatever the gun was, the bullets didn't penetrate the door, which meant they probably wouldn't penetrate my fancy duster.

It didn't last. Three men drew their weapons as I entered the passenger car. The scientist ducked behind the seats, and it seemed like a good call. Heaving the door in front of me, I stepped to the side. Another shot came from Casket, winging one of his men. The man swore but Casket kept firing.

"Well," I said to the scientist. "Any ideas?"

Reginald shook his head. His glasses were falling off the bridge of his nose, and he didn't bother to fix them. He drew his knees up to his chest and hugged them—a truly hopeless gesture for anyone trying to escape a speeding train.

"We'll get out of here," I said, not really believing it. Without my guns, my odds were slim, and the way my hand still throbbed, guns wouldn't do me much good anyway. I needed a plan.

Pulling my bulletproof coat tight around me, I stood up, raising my hands in the air. "Listen, I—"

They shot me. Three horse kicks pounded my chest at once, sending me crashing into the wall. The door fell from my hand, and a boil of outrage burned in my belly. Without bothering to check if any of the bullets had penetrated, I scooped up the door again, roared my most furious roar, and charged down the aisle.

I suppose I must have felt the bullets hit me from behind. It doesn't seem possible that I didn't feel something clip through my coat and bounce off my ribs. Not even a little. The three men in front didn't hit, though. I tossed the door at one, crushing him against the wall. The guy on the right stumbled backward, tripping over a seat. I grabbed the middle guy's gun, hand, and wrist in my big metal fist and crushed all three into a mess.

The guy on the right started to recover, but I planted a bloody boot in his face hard enough to hear the crack-snap of bone.

Bloody? Why was my boot bloody? No time to think about it, so I turned back to Casket Jones, who was still two cars away, trapped under the door I'd thrown at him. That explained why he didn't follow. He raised his shining red revolver at me, shark grin plastered on his tumored face. Our eyes met for one long breath, and in his gaze I saw the downfall of all Texas. That burning hatred I'd felt so often for the criminals of my town—I saw that in his broken features. He was a madman, but a madman full of righteous fury—a fury I myself could no longer muster in my too-often burned soul.

I couldn't match this man. I probably couldn't even escape.

His arm tensed, he aimed at my head. It'd be a clean kill, anyway. No need to bleed out.

Then the train banked around a bend, and he disappeared from view. I swept the scientist forward, not bothering to ask permission. Together we pushed into the next car. The luggage train with Francis's coffin. I jammed my extra door up against the one we'd just passed through, wedging it shut. It wouldn't stop anyone for long, but hopefully it would buy us some time.

My human hand was twisted into a claw by pain and injury, but I knew what I needed to do next. The necessity of it burned like bile in my belly. It hurt more than the keening ache I now felt through my whole body. I slammed my open hand onto the access panel of Francis's coffin, swearing at the fresh wave of pain. The device powered up.

The door to the next car slid open, and a man walked in with a shotgun. Without thinking, I shoved the coffin hard with my big hand, and it hit the guy in the knees. Something crunched in his legs, and he tumbled backward through the door.

Reginald rushed to the panel and shut the man out, locking the cargo car from the inside. "You have a minute," he said.

"I need two," I said. "And we need to slow down the train."

He shook his head. "I don't know how to take control of the train."

"No, but I know someone who does."

The coffin floated an inch above the train floor, and every bend in the tracks caused it to shift. On its controls, a bloody handprint highlighted the touchscreen. Where had all that blood come from?

I dropped to a knee. The pain faded, like a cold, numbing claw grasping my heart. I punched my code into the coffin, and the thing hissed open. Deep asleep, Francis lay there, his open eyes wet as if from tears. His chest rose and fell, and unconscious tension simmered beneath his otherwise serene expression.

"I can't believe I'm doing this," I muttered.

With three quick punches at the controls, I woke Francis William Brown from his coma. His eyes snapped open, and he sat up. He looked around, his face a mask of confusion and fear—emotions I'd never before seen on his fine features. The effect was appalling, and my own heart pounded in my chest with a mix of fear and empathy.

"What's happening?" he asked. His voice cracked.

I grabbed a handful of his shirt and pulled him close. "You gotta stop the train."

His eyes met mine for a hundred rapid heartbeats, and I thought maybe the coffin had done something terrible to him. That he might come out a different man than he'd gone in. Then his features smoothed over, and the coldly rational Francis that I knew returned for a fraction of a second. He looked from me to Reginald, and then up at the ceiling. His breaths slowed, but the tension of raw emotion still made the muscles of his jaw twitch.

"A train," he said. "Good."

"You gotta slow it," I told him.

He nodded. Closing his eyes, he raised his hands up, palms out. Francis's brain had been more computer than soft bits since he was a little kid. If anyone could hack the wireless controls for the bullet train, it would be him. Only question was whether he could do it fast enough.

The scientist cowered in the corner, trying to make himself

small. I pulled him forward and piled him onto Francis's coffin. "Hold tight," I said. He looked at me like I was off my rocker.

He might have been right.

The train jerked, sending me flying off my feet, hitting the wall hard. It braked hard, and the hum through the floor became an urgent scream. I fought the pull and swung my arm up fast enough to catch the coffin as it slid at me. My eyes met the scientist's, and I must have looked terrible because my grin set him to fits of panicked breath.

"I said hold tight," I told him.

When his soft hands had finally found a good grip on the edges of the open coffin, I punched through the emergency release button's protective case on the cargo car's wall and jumped in next to him. The whole wall and ceiling of the car split wide open, peeling like tissue paper in the fierce wind. We'd slowed but not enough.

But it was too late. The floating coffin, along with two thirds of their crates, flew out the hatch, into the harsh Texan landscape, and over a cliff into a canyon.

8

Of all the flying contraptions folks have built over the years, the one I would recommend to wary travelers the absolute least is the flying coffin.

Weightless.

With all the Texas wastes stretched out before me, the sound of my own whooping scream rang loud in my ears. Reginald clutched my arm so hard his fingernails cut through the bone-thick haze of numbness that washed through me. Francis's eye glazed over, watery like a pond on a still winter day.

Coffins, even those with built-in gravity drives, lacked something in precision. This one had two modes, "On," and "Off." "On" wasn't doing us a whole hell of a lot of good, but it was significantly better than the alternative.

It wasn't good enough.

The world stayed weightless for several thousand thumps of my panicked heart. We hovered, suspended above the cracked desert canyons drifting away from the speeding train. Far off in the distance, the burned forests stood watch at the base of blue-black mountains. As we sped through the dry hot air, pushed by our own momentum, the world below us spun in the blistering morning sun. Below, precious cargo spilled across the ravaged land, broken by the staggering steep drop that we ourselves would soon enjoy.

Not that we were much looking forward to it. The coffin tipped, and the little scientist screamed. I pulled on the edge and leaned, righting the coffin. What good it would do, I couldn't tell.

Francis blinked, his eyes snapping into focus. He saw me and he wept. My gut wrenched at the sight of him, despite myself. His shoulders shook and a low, keening cry bubbled from somewhere deep in his throat.

"The coffin will lower us," I shouted over the rush of wind.

He looked down at the black claws of his hands, their artificial fingers clutched into claws. He was the picture of pain, worse than any raw emotion I'd ever seen in another man.

Then the coffin started to drop. It wasn't made for three passengers, even if Francis and Reginald weren't anywhere near its rated capacity. The stupid device was programmed to float close to the earth, and its little computer was probably throwing an absolute fit about the hundreds of meters we'd achieved in our one quick blast over the cliff.

Then Francis blinked at me again, his eyes absolutely unconcerned.

"Don't get too comfy," I told him. "You're going back under when we land." But my voice came out as a weak rasp. Something felt wrong in my chest. "But I need your help right now, Francis."

"It's Frank," he said, barely audible over the rush of wind.

Frank. I remembered the first day I'd met him, on the day his father died. He'd said his name was Frank, but idiot I was, I'd always called him Francis. "You want to live through this, Francis?"

Reginald let out something that sounded like a cross between a scream and the bleat of a goat.

"We're not going to make it," Francis said. "It can't handle this."

I hazarded a glance over the edge. The ground below approached at an alarming speed. "We're fine."

"No." Francis reached for the controls, but I smacked his hand away. His eyes didn't leave the controls to bother looking at me. "I can save us."

"Or you might kill us all." If I gave him access to the coffin's systems, it would never be safe from him.

This time he looked at me. A shred of unidentifiable emotion slipped across his face. "Have you ever known me to be suicidal, J.D.?"

I hadn't. "Promise you'll submit once we're on the ground."

"No."

My hat threatened to fly off my head. Air rushed past faster and faster, ground rushing closer. We'd hit in seconds.

"Fine!" I shouted.

"Hold on," he said. His fingers flew across the controls. A wave of gravity pulsed all around us—wrenched at my gut like I was being twisted by a giant. The scientist passed out. The machine squealed. A horrid black smoke belched from somewhere under the slick white panels.

And we dropped like a rock. True weightlessness tugged at my gut, unencumbered by the gravity drive that should have been slowing us. I had time to shoot Francis the dirtiest of scowls before he mashed the controls again and the coffin slowed.

Not enough.

We hit hard and the edge of the coffin snapped up to slam me in the face. I flew free, black spots swallowing the bright day. I gasped for sweet breath, unable to draw so much as a mouthful of air. The whole world blossomed in pain for nobody knows how long. A fire burned somewhere, and for a hundred shallow, painful breaths, I couldn't even say if it was me.

Then the sun blotted out into a deep shadow.

"Thanks for letting me go," Francis said, the sun making a silhouette of him. "You did the right thing. Too bad if it's the last thing you do."

"Always kinda figured it would be," I said when my breath had come back enough. Everything ached in my poor, old body. The bullet wounds I'd suffered on the train finally saw fit to make themselves known. My morbid brain idly wondered how this would go. Would Francis leave me to bleed out in the desert? Or would he play it safe and finish me off before leaving? Which option was more logical?

I felt his arms in my armpits as he dragged me into the shade of a rock that looked something like a twisted bison. The air cooled in that dark space, but then again, everything felt cold. Damn cold. A minute or maybe hours later, Francis plopped Reginald down next to me. The little man was unconscious but still breathing.

"Francis," I said before dissolving into a wracking cough.

"Be still," he said. He stood there, the bright sun shining off his white hair. His pallid skin cut the light like a ceramic knife against the clear blue sky.

I was still for a while, though not entirely by choice. My body refused to comply, and a great weakness washed over me. Through it all, my metal arm continued at full strength, unhindered by my lost blood or impending death. I wondered what would happen to the damn thing. Would it be the only part of me to survive, wandering the wasteland hunting criminals in the vast nothing that Texas would one day become? Part of me hoped it would be true.

Part of me wondered if that's what had happened to Francis. Had the metal parts of him continued on after the fleshy bits had long since died? Or was that same innocent kid still riding along inside that head of his?

I'd killed his mother right in front of him. The boy had

always been strange, but he hadn't always been broken. That day, with the monstrous storm and his crazed mother, had he finally snapped? Was that when the boy Francis fell away and the machine mind took over? Maybe the same thing had happened to Texas itself long ago too. The humanity sloughed off like rotten meat from a bone, leaving nothing but the technological skeleton to dance under a cursed star.

"Why are you laughing?" Francis asked.

I shook my head. "We're all the same, you know."

After a long pause, he said, "Your friends will be here soon. Just hang on until then."

Despite the pain, my laugh grew into an honest-to-goodness guffaw.

"What?"

"Friends," I said. "You think I have friends."

"Sheriff—"

"I haven't been a sheriff for a long time, son."

"And I haven't been a son for right about just as long. We all carry echoes of who we used to be, don't we?"

When I raised my hand to take off my hat, I saw that three of my fingers had swollen into large purple sausages. "I suppose we do," I said, lowering my arm.

Time might've passed. It did that thing where it stands still forever, and suddenly the sun is low in the horizon. A far-off loping sound echoed through the ravine, and a few minutes later I was being loaded into the back of a long van.

I heard a woman's voice. "He'll live, if that's what you want."

And to my surprise, Francis answered, "Yes."

9

―――――

The smell of charred brisket woke me with a start, accompanied by a whole bucket of bad memories. My mouth tasted of dry Texas desert and my heart pounded like the hoofbeats of a panicked horse. It was dark, and the only sound was the parched, staccato rasp of my own breath.

All the world hurt.

A door opened in the black, and blue light shone in from the other room. "You okay in there?" said a woman—the same woman who had picked us up from the desert.

"Fine," I said, trying to sit up. First thing I noticed was the articulated black cast on my right hand. It allowed for some stiff movement of my fingers, but otherwise held all the bones in place.

Second thing I noticed was the lack of balance that came from blood loss. I lay back down.

She crossed to my bedside, easing me back into position. The woman had strong hands, and I almost wanted to relax. From the light still seeping in through the door, I recognized her. "Rosa," I said. It was her, older now, but I'm not one to hold that against a person. Her skin was a deeper bronze, and laugh lines had started forming at the corners of her eyes. Was this the friend Francis called for me? Why not Trish?

Did Francis even know about Trish?

Of course he did. Trish had a bounty out on his head. That wasn't something Francis was likely to miss. He'd know her exact location seconds after waking up in that coffin. Damn, why did I wake him up? My sluggish brain wrapped itself around the details of the previous day.

Rosa must have seen the look on my face. "Legs and I have a place out here. Far enough from Candlestick Crossing to avoid most of the trouble. Close enough to still get some business done."

"Smart," I said. Couldn't think of anything else.

She flashed a knowing smile. There was more she wasn't telling me, but I was too exhausted to get it out of her. Instead, I lay back and let the bed swallow me.

When I woke, thin sunlight filtered into the room through a haze of dust. I forced myself up, taking account of the new holes in my bare chest. Casket Jones must have shot me with something that pierced straight through my bulletproof coat. Every shot had speared right through me, leaving a tiny exit wound. I counted six holes in all. A miracle I'd survived, really. An ache in my ribs told me that maybe one or two shots had bounced off bone, but I suspect nothing was broken.

My hand was another matter. The cast still held in place, and I could see my purple fingers poking out the end.

Using my metal arm to steady myself, I stood. The room swayed, but I'd recovered significantly. Blood nannies would help with that. Army issued tech wasn't bad back when I got my arm installed. It'd saved my life a dozen times before, so I wasn't concerned about giving it a workout. The tech quickened my healing, purged toxins, and fought infection. Even *I* had to admit that was handy.

The room was a bedroom with wooden walls and drab fixtures. I'd bled on the bed, for which I was sorry. There was a lone dresser, with a small lamp. The only decoration in the whole room was a white man's Jesus in a small oil painting. I didn't know how I felt about white Jesus watching over me as I slept. On the dresser sat a black shirt about my size, so I pulled it over my head. It had a print of a bison skull on the front. It'd be a while before I could go back to wearing the button-down shirts I preferred, so I resigned myself to wearing the stylish threads of a much younger man.

I pushed my way into the other room and was immediately greeted by a "Ha!" from Legs followed by a quick exchange of stars between him and Rosa. They both sat at a small card table, with the remains of eggs, toast, and coffee.

"You had a bet if I'd make it?" I asked, eyeing the coffee. I wasn't sure I could pour myself some in my current state.

Legs, a man with golden skin covered in twisting tattoos, grinned. He'd changed a lot since last I saw him. He'd bulked up, modified even more of his body with sleek, golden tech, and he'd grown out his hair. He almost looked like an adult. "I bet you'd be up before noon. It's eleven forty-five."

Rosa scowled. "He also bet that you'd die before sunset."

"I could still win that one."

Legs rose in a single smooth motion. He had always been a fan of augmented legs, and he now had legs that segmented into four so that he walked like a spider. When he appeared to be sitting at the table, he was really resting back on folded legs. When he stood, the legs joined, and he walked like a good old-fashioned human being—but taller. He stood a good dozen centimeters taller than me. Made me feel like a damn kid.

I stuck my hand out to shake his, but then realized it would be hard with all my bandages. He rescued the awkward situation by pulling me into a hard hug. The squeeze hurt like hell on my chest, but when he finally let up, the sense of connection lingered. It'd been a long time since I'd last seen Legs. Even longer since I'd first chased him down the street like the criminal he was.

Rosa poured me a cup of coffee and I sat at the table. Awkwardly, my left hand brought the cup to my lips and the coffee tasted better than any whiskey I'd ever drank. The burned, bitter flavor woke my senses up and when I looked down I discovered I'd finished the whole cup. Rosa poured another.

"Not sure I should drink too much," I said, looking down at my bandaged hand. "Gonna be hard to piss."

Legs let out a sharp laugh. "You're so dehydrated, I don't think you have to worry about that at all before you kick off later this afternoon."

"What's with the fancy bandage, anyway?" I asked Rosa. "My nannies should have me knit up by now."

She shook her head. "It's in a bad state. Nannies are trying to heal it wrong, so I had to pin the bones in place and try to reprogram them."

My mouth went dry again. Badly programmed nannies were a mess of a way to die. "Any luck?"

She shot a nervous glance at Legs that I failed to miss. "Should be okay if you keep that out of trouble for the next few days."

"You don't think I will?"

She shook her head. Instead of answering, she left the little kitchen through a screen door. Legs fried me some eggs, which I gratefully devoured. They sat lumpy in my stomach, but the flavor and the salt felt good on my lips. I almost started to feel alive again before Rosa came back in with Reginald in tow.

"You've met Reginald?" Rosa asked, gesturing at the little man.

"Sure," I said.

The little scientist stuck out his hand as if to shake mine. "Reginald White," he said. "Thank you so much for saving me." Then he realized I wouldn't shake his hand and withdrew the offer.

I took a sip of coffee. "Hell of a situation you had yourself in."

Rosa put an arm around the fella like they were old friends. "Why don't you tell him what you were doing on that train?"

"I know what he was doing," I said. "What made them think you're qualified to make biological weaponry?"

Reginald went two shades paler. "They picked me up just this side of the Canadian border, over by the coast. There's a research facility out there where we work with the old diseases and their cures." He looked at me as if expecting a question. When he didn't get it, he continued. "Typhoid, smallpox, syphilis, rabies. That last one's of particular interest. You know it crosses the blood-brain barrier? They use it to install certain kinds of replicating nanotech."

"Sure," I said. I hadn't heard anything about it, but what he was saying made sense.

"Well, those fellas on the train got a sample of a rabies variant that we considered an abject failure in our labs. It tested so poorly on rats we burned the whole line of inquiry."

My stomach churned. "So you decided to sell it as a weapon."

Reginald's eyes went wide. "It wasn't me, I—"

"Chester Goodwin thinks he has a way to win the war," said a voice behind me. I turned to see Francis standing there: a dark, ragged shadow in the doorway.

The coffee cup shattered in my metal hand. "What the hell are you doing here?"

Francis stepped inside the kitchen. Suddenly the room felt crowded and close. "I couldn't pass up the opportunity to taunt you when you're weak, could I?" The words lacked any playfulness that might have made the statement teasing or fun. Even so, Francis didn't come across as awkward and stilted as he usually did. Nor was he the blubbering mess that stepped out of that coffin.

"I could still kill you," I said.

"You don't have your guns or knives. A long as I'm out of arm's reach, I'm fine." He leaned up against the doorframe, arms crossed.

He was right. Even if I lunged for him across the room and somehow caught him, I was no match. Hell, I'd be lucky to ever get back to fighting shape the way I felt. Seemed to me Legs had made a pretty solid bet.

"So Goodwin has a new weapon, then," I said. "But why's Casket Jones working for the corporates? Jones tried to recruit me for a rebellion."

Reginald shook his head. "Jones is a bounty hunter over anything else. If the payday's high enough, he'll deliver whatever Goodwin wants."

"Including me," Francis said. "I helped him acquire the virus."

"And he crippled you so you'd be easy to catch."

Reginald continued. "He made me engineer the stable delivery mechanism for the disease. Goodwin might have been his target."

My head throbbed. Rose poured me another coffee, and I carefully took a sip. My gut told me that something didn't add up, but my head wasn't in any shape to figure out what. "I suppose they're long gone, then."

Legs grinned. "You busted up a pile of their cargo, hoss. They're still out there trying to gather it up."

Reginald said, "They'll have trouble keeping the virus viable. The lab is basically worthless without me. I was only ever able to make seven stable delivery units."

"How long will it take them to gather up what they need?" I asked.

Rosa said, "That's the thing. They should be done already."

"The virus is extremely unstable in culture," Reginald said. "They'll want to move as soon as possible if they have it."

I scratched at my beard. "What if they infected someone with it? Could that keep it alive?"

Reginald paled. "You should bomb the train if you can. This can't get out."

"What's near there?" I asked. "Any towns with livestock they can use?"

"They can't just use anything. It would have to be humans." Reginald ran his fingers through his thinning hair. "The blood or saliva of infected people would be enough to spread the virus. But..."

"What?" I growled.

"The virus doesn't behave well with implanted tech."

"They'll use people who can't afford implants," I said. "Or people who are philosophically opposed."

"Correct."

"How long will it take them before the train gets moving?" I asked.

"I don't know," said Reginald. "If they've gathered up the cargo already, then they must be looking for me—or Francis."

"I covered our tracks," Francis said.

"How long will it take them?" I growled.

Francis's eyes flashed violet. "I left false leads that they could follow for days." He looked straight at me. "Trust me, I can lead a hunter around on a wild chase for a long damn time. They won't find this place."

Legs said. "If they're just gathering up people and infecting them, they'll raid the settlements around that area."

I forced myself to my feet. The coffee had fortified me some, and I was able to move on my own without help. "Legs, Reginald, you stay here and figure out where they'll find people if they're going to do that. Hinder them if you can. Rosa, I need you to take me back to Crossing."

"What for?" she asked.

I looked at each of them in turn. Francis wouldn't meet my gaze, but each of the others looked back with a kind of stiff defiance. These were hard people, made harder by their lives in the wastelands of Texas. I'd never ask them to do more than needed, but we had to do what we had to do.

"We're putting together a gang," I said. "If we want to rob that train, then I need to go recruit some help."

10

———

The sun sat hot and lazy in the afternoon sky by the time Rosa landed her massive van next to the Candle at the edge of Candlestick Crossing. Her deft hand at the controls set us down in a puff of dust with nothing more than a light thump. With some difficulty, I climbed down from the passenger seat, my boots hitting the dry earth.

Rosa circled looked me over. "You going to make it?"

"I'll be fine." A lie. "This place is just too damn friendly during the day."

"It's friendly enough at night too," Rosa said. She rubbed her finger and thumb together. "But it costs you."

"Costs you just as much during the day.

The Crossing was the only place I knew for a hundred kilometers that would have the quality of person I was looking for. I didn't need the kind of gunslinger who stayed home and protected her land. Didn't matter how quick a person was or how deadly they were with their chosen weapon. What I needed was someone who knew how to sling bullets and had a certain willingness to not discriminate about the targets.

Specifically, I was looking to hire Sunset and her gang.

"Trish!" I hollered when we were in front of the motel. Muffin stood tied out front, so I knew Trish and Quin couldn't be far. I greeted my horse, careful even after all these years not to sneak up on her. "Hey, girl," I said, rubbing her flank.

Trish stepped out of the hotel room, Quin close on her heels.

"We figured you were dead," Quin said.

The sheriff shook her head. "J.D.'s too stubborn to die."

"There's something big going down," I said to Trish.

"There always is." She took a step forward to place a hand on Muffin. "Like the something you told me to stay out of around here."

"Did you?"

"Mostly." Then she saw Rosa.

Their guns were out faster than a man could blink. Quin ducked back into the hotel room, and Trish's eyes flashed in the afternoon light.

"What the fuck?" Rosa said. "This is the help you were looking for?"

"Rosa Garcia," Trish shouted. "There is a warrant for your arrest."

I raised my hands, palm out, and stepped between the two women. "Now hold on."

Trish said, "Get back, J.D."

"This bitch isn't going to help us, old man," Rosa said. "She fucking killed Legs's cousin."

"She'll help," I said, directing the comment at Trish. "Once she knows—"

Rosa stepped up behind me, using my bulk as cover. Her gun, a stubby black revolver that smelled of fresh oil and clean efficiency stuck pointed at Trish like an accusation.

"Trish," I said, using my most calming voice. "Put your guns down. Rosa, you too. We got bigger cattle to rustle."

Trish hazarded a glance at me. "Stay out of this."

"Rosa's a friend," I said.

"Friend?" Rosa said, incredulous. "Really?"

"Acquaintance."

Rosa nodded. "Barely."

"We gotta get back on that train, Trish," I said.

"Like hell you do." Trish said, sidestepping to use the horse for better cover. "Where's Francis?"

"She's here to help," I said, "And Rosa, I said put your gun down. Trish isn't going to drag you in."

"I'm not?"

"You're not."

Rosa took a step back, making sure I still blocked Trish's shot. "This is bullshit."

"It's not," I said, turning around to face her.

She met my gaze for several heartbeats. There was fear in her eyes, and something like real pain fighting against those laugh lines.

Rosa retreated back to her van. When I turned back to Trish, she already had her pistols holstered and one hell of a scowl on her face.

We went into the tiny hotel room. Quin pressed herself as far back into the corner as she could, peering at me with blood-shot eyes. The wall in the back still ventilated the whole place with a massive square hole. The room dripped with tension, and I didn't even have the first clue how to cut it.

"There's a plague on that train," I said.

That didn't do it. The two women stared at me like I was talking like a damn fool.

"We thought you were dead," Quin said. Her face was blotchy, and her hair looked like it'd exploded. "*I* thought you were dead."

"He might still be," Trish said, anger rumbling beneath the smooth tones of her voice.

"You never liked me much," I said.

Quin's jaw hardened. I didn't know why she cared so much

about me. We'd hardly traveled together for very long. There wasn't any reason she should still be with me at all, since I'd lost Francis.

I stepped closer. "Look—"

"What happened to you?" Trish asked, eyeing my ruined right hand in its cast. "And why are you wearing that shirt?"

"Casket Jones has a bioweapon, Trish."

She took a step closer, peering at me. "You've been shot."

"He's going to—"

"I think you should arrest him," Quin interjected.

"Me?" I raised my hands in protest. "Now, hold on."

"Not worth it," Trish said. "We should shoot him."

"Wait—"

Quin stood. "You had a whole day to call us."

My knees went weak. After all that, there wasn't anything left in me. Before I really understood what was happening, I sat hard on the corner of the bed. The whole room spun around me like I'd been drinking whiskeys all night. "I need to get back on that train," I said.

Quin perked up. "A train heist?"

I said, "No, it's—"

Trish stepped forward. "Maybe I should arrest you right now."

"No—" I couldn't concentrate. "I'm not here for you."

"We thought you were dead, J.D.," Trish said. "When that train left…"

"This is more important than all that." What business did they have worrying about me, anyway? I tried to rub the exhaustion from my eyes with the back of my cast. It didn't help. "This is a bioweapon. A bad one. Jones means to hit the city with it."

Trish said nothing for a long time, her expression unreadable. "The train is the only way into Austin these days."

"And Casket knows it."

Quin finally broke her silence. "I'm in."

Trish's shoulders relaxed. "Fine. I'll help." *My gut tells me she's not saying something.*

They both looked at me, as if awaiting my approval. I held the gaze of each, making sure they met me back. It was a hard road we were going to travel, and I wasn't going to let either of them travel it without knowing the gravity of the situation, especially the kid.

"I'm not here to recruit you," I said. "This is a bad mission, right through the middle."

Quin smiled. "We'll let you tag along, anyway."

"Okay," I said. "Let's load Muffin into Rosa's hauler. There's one more person I want to have a chat with."

"I'm going to arrest her, J.D.," Trish said.

"After."

She nodded.

"Good enough." *We'd cross that desert when we stumbled on it.*

"No, it's not really good enough, but it's what we're getting, isn't it?" Trish said. "Seems you've been getting in my way a lot lately."

Fair enough. First Court, then Rosa. How many other criminals would I need to protect from Trish? "Just trying to do the right thing." *I wasn't sure how much that was true.*

Rosa was atop her van, using its position to get a good vantage of the surrounding area. She saw us coming, and if the little snubnosed revolver she carried had been a threat, then the rifle she held loosely at her side was an all-out declaration of war. Trish and Quin stayed far away and around the corner while I approached.

"Sheriff's not coming after you," I said as I approached the van. "Not today, anyway."

Rosa said, "What makes you think I'm not coming after her?"

"Because you're the smart one, Rosa. You always were."

She muttered a curse under her breath and got out to open the back of the van. There was plenty of room back there for a horse or two. Muffin wasn't exactly thrilled, but with a few sweet words, we got her loaded up.

I sidled over to the little tavern. Inside, I found half a dozen people drinking whiskey and beer. A trio sat at a table playing poker, and one of them perked up soon as I entered. It was the gangly man I'd hogtied outside the bear's cave. His expression lacked the appreciation for all that mercy I'd shown him.

I bellied up to the bar, next to a massive figure whose bright clothes lit up the darkened room. As I lowered myself gingerly onto a stool, I groaned at the aches in all my joints and said, "I feel like I wrestled a damn bear."

Sunset swallowed the remains of her whiskey and turned slowly to me. "Is this a callout, J.D.? This going to be a guns-at-noon kind of thing? You still mad I tried to steal your bounty?"

The gangly man stood up from the poker table. Another one followed.

"Mad?" I considered it for a long, painful breath. "No, I'm not mad. I understand a person gets desperate sometimes."

She hissed. With the wave of a finger, she summoned two more whiskeys. She pushed one to me. "Well, I'm sorry." Eyeing me up, she said, "You *look* like you wrestled a bear."

"Hey!" The gangly man grabbed my shoulder and pulled me around. His breath reeked of cheap booze. "You're that asshole."

"This ain't a callout," I said, not sure if I could disarm the situation. "I just want to chat with your boss."

His grin was missing a few teeth. My hand throbbed at the memory of slugging him back by the cave. That was the first time I'd broken that hand. I ought to be more careful with it. His buddy, the other guy I'd abused at the cave, crossed his arms.

"Now gentlemen—"

Gangly took his first swing faster than I'd expected. Fast but clumsy. I rolled with it, deflecting most of the blow. I almost had a hand up when the other guy punched hard at my bruised ribs. Flares of molten pain burst in my chest. A fire lit in my belly and before I could blink, rage snapped me back into fighting shape.

A backhand from the metal arm sent the gangly fella flying. His buddy tried another gut punch, but I deflected it with my cast—not a great idea. My fingers went numb, but I shoved the damn cast back in his face and punched low with my metal arm.

"I don't want any trouble," I said.

Gangly tackled me hard from the side. The two of us toppled over, crashing into a table.

I rolled, landed on top, and slammed his head hard into the floor. When he didn't move, I stood, leveling my best glare at the second guy. I slowly, carefully clenched my metal hand into a fist, letting the gritty joints grind loudly as I did.

The guy turned tail and was out before I could blink.

With the blood loss and the damage my nannies had taken, the whiskey in front of me might have actually messed some with my head. The temptation to pound it back and follow it up with a half dozen more was almost unbearable, but I pushed it over to Sunset. She raised an eyebrow.

"Round one with the bear didn't go so well," I said. "I'm looking for some support on round two."

"Who's the bear?"

Here, I paused for a long time. I didn't know how Sunset got along with Casket Jones, but stepping on bounty hunter territories could be a complex road to a slit neck. If she didn't agree to help me, rumor might get out that I was hunting Jones. What little support I had would dissolve and I'd find myself bleeding in a ditch in no time. Bounty hunters had a twisted version of honor that tended to reinforce itself with a knife in the back or a boot to the head.

"We're going to rob a train," I said.

She slammed back one of the whiskeys. "I'm a bounty hunter, J.D. I don't rob trains, I catch people."

We sat in silence for a long time while the quietly crude activity of the bar bustled around us. Some new players at the poker table swore and cursed, and a pair playing darts told bad jokes. Several more rough customers filtered in from the hot afternoon sun.

I considered it a moment. "If the law sees proof someone's transporting bioweapons there'll be a bounty before you can spit. All I'm askin' for is your company while we wait for that to come along."

"Who's the target?"

"Casket Jones."

Sunset scoffed. "That bastard *is* a bioweapon."

"If you're the closest when the bounty lands on his head, you'll be the first to get a crack at him. He's all yours. No need to poach."

"It wasn't poaching. I was chasing a different bounty contract," she said. "One that said to bring Francis Brown in dead."

So that was the loophole she'd used to justify her attack. Valid enough, I suppose.

Sunset drank back the second whiskey. "I'm in." She shot a glance down to Gangly, where he moaned on the floor. "But my gang needs a break."

"For the best," I said. "Wait till you see who else is on the team."

11

———

Under the waning light of a half moon, the broken landscape around Legs and Rosa's home was a washed-out blue watercolor sprinkled with the pinprick stars in the clear sky. I sat on a boulder still warm from the day's sun, wearing my long duster over the bison skull shirt. The cool breeze blew through the new bullet holes in the coat, testament to the limits of its bulletproof nature. One more thing betraying its one and only purpose in the world.

"No evidence of raids on the towns around the train," said Legs. "But the train hasn't moved yet."

"What are they waiting for?"

Legs shrugged as he walked away. "Maybe they're waiting for you."

A short distance away, Sunset spoke with Trish.

"There's a rhythm to it," Trish said, pointing her twin pistols at the unseen distance. "Aim both targets, then boom-boom. Aim. Boom-boom. Both pistols are the same, so your brain doesn't have to do a lot of work differentiating."

"I don't know," Sunset said. "I always learned to keep one

weapon as the main, with a second for backup if I ran out of ammo."

Trish holstered one of her silver pistols and ejected the cartridge from the other. "I always say if I'm in a fight that takes more than twenty-four bullets per gun, with no time for a proper reload, then I probably screwed something up along the way."

Sunset barked out a laugh. The two women took swigs from the same vodka bottle, and hell if it wasn't actually starting to affect them. "I'm positive we're fixin' to walk into exactly that situation."

"How do you do it, Sun? You always bring in any bounty I post, and you're quicker than anyone out there."

Sunset nodded at Francis, who sat cross-legged in a swinging chair by the house. "What do you want him alive for? We'd do the world a favor putting a bullet in that skull."

"Everyone gets a trial," Trish said, her voice flat. "Even the butcher of Swallow Hill."

"Still."

"We'll worry about Brown when the train is taken care of. I checked out the Reginald guy's references. The lab he's from is real, and I think he's telling the truth about how dangerous it is."

"But why the bounty on Francis now? That whole Swallow Hill business was a long time ago."

Trish took a long pull of vodka, finishing off the bottle. She said, "Think quick," and tossed it high in the air.

Sunset drew and fired. A single shot rang out in the night, and molten glass rained across the dry earth. Trish whooped. I'd never seen her so damn happy with someone. The two women wandered off, no doubt in search of more booze.

"Hey," Quin said, sliding up next to me on the boulder a short while later.

"Hey." After a long silence, I finally said, "Sorry."

"It's okay."

"I shouldn't have let that train start moving. You could have been abandoned in that town, and I'm not sure a kid like you would have survived."

"I'm not a kid."

I gave her a hard look. "You're close enough."

She looked like she was biting back words. "I'm going to help you stop that train."

"Sure," I said. "Like you said, you're not a kid. No responsibility of mine."

"None, huh?"

"None."

"Then why do you wince every time I talk about doing something dangerous?"

I stuck a thumb out at the house, where Francis sat with glowing eyes. "I tried to protect Francis once. Look how he turned out. It doesn't matter if I fight or if I lay down and die. Texas chews kids up and spits them out onto the hard red dirt." It came out much harsher than I'd intended.

After a long pause, she said, "The sheriff says you don't know how to *not* fight."

"I suppose that's true." Why did I care so much about the train and its bioweapon? Did it matter all that much to me if someone unleashed a disease on Austin? On Dead Oak? Either way, it'd mean chaos, but what did that matter to me? "Truth is, I never stopped caring about my people. All of my people. The kids, the ranchers, even the criminals. They were mine to protect, and I put every gram of my soul into doing it. Even though they don't need me no more, and even though I'm more of a wanted man than a lawman, I fight every damn day to make their lives better. If I didn't have that, I wouldn't have anything."

"You could, though," Quin said.

I tipped my hat to her and slid down off the boulder. My knees ached and when my arm got jostled hot iron pain ran up the tendons. I'd go fight in the morning, even if I wasn't going to be of much use. I'd barely escaped last time.

Muffin had a long acreage out back of the house. When I went to see her, she was a fair way off, so I walked out and patted her on the cheek.

"You'll be here a bit," I said to her. "Maybe a good long while, if things don't go well."

She nuzzled my coat, trying to pull open the pocket where I kept the sugar cubes. I relented, as I always did, and gave her one. Rubbing her down one last time before heading back to the house.

Inside the house, Legs and Rosa sat at the table, where a map of the area was projected in a three-dimensional rendering. The images were updated with the exact location of the train and the positions of their workers.

"J.D.," said Rosa, "tell this asshole we can't just blow the whole thing up."

"It's the safest way," Legs said. "Even the scientist agrees."

I eased myself into a chair at the table. "Since when does safety matter to you?"

Legs went quiet, leaning back in a chair made of his oddly folded legs.

"Look," Rosa said, "We fly in at first light, using the sun to blind sensors on our way in. If we hit the train in back first, all we have to do is move along the top and hit the cars that Reggie tagged for us." In the projected image, three of the cars glowed red. "We steal what we want from those and burn whatever we don't take. Profit, victory, and maybe a little revenge—whatever's your game."

"Justice," Trish said as she entered. Sunset followed, with Reginald in tow.

Rosa shot her a look, then shifted her seat so as not to turn her back on the lawwoman. "Sure," she said. "Justice and honor and all that."

Legs pressed his lips together.

"What are we looking for?" I asked after reviewing her plan. It was a solid one, but there were details left out.

"Seven cases," Rosa said. She pulled up an image of a black case with a stylized coyote on the front.

I remembered seeing those cases on the train. "Only seven?"

Reginald said, "Everything else has probably already died off without me maintaining it."

"Unless they infect people with those doses," I said.

Legs shook his head. "We've been watching the area. They haven't gathered anybody."

I took off my hat and set it on the table, disrupting their projected image. The disturbance shifted the image along the tracks, bringing it to a more familiar territory.

"Is that Dead Oak?" I asked.

The tracks ran right up to my old stomping grounds. Then, after passing through a long ravine, the tracks ran straight past the Brown Ranch where they disappeared under a tunnel for several kilometers. These tracks hadn't existed when I'd been sheriff. When had anyone started building new tracks?

Rosa took my broken hand in hers. Slowly, and with tender care I hadn't felt in years, she disengaged my cast one section at a time. "We could drop you off there, you know. Dead Oak isn't in as bad a shape as a lot of the other towns, and you don't really need to be a part of this."

The offer was tempting. It had been years since I'd visited that town, and every nerve in my body told me it was time for retirement. "All I heard was the war's tearing everything apart."

"It is, but Dead Oak's got better resources than most. Better organization."

"They have Trish."

"They do." She spat it Trish's direction like a curse. What had she tried to get away with in Trish's town? "And all trade with Austin runs through town."

Rosa pulled my cast off, revealing my mottled, ugly wreck of a hand. It had healed well enough, but the ravages of the injury still showed in yellow and black bruises and oddly shaped lumps where my joints had once been normal. I clenched a fist, defying the crackle of pain as I did.

"Good as new," I said through gritted teeth.

Legs let out a nervous laugh. "You could go for a replacement."

I shot him a hell of a scowl.

Rosa shrugged, looking genuinely apologetic. "Best I could do," she said. It'll keep healing as long as you don't wreck it again."

But I wasn't listening. I still stared at Dead Oak on the little map. How long had it been since I'd visited that little town? It still held a special place in my heart. Just seeing it on the miniature projection made my heart race like a man seeing the face of his lover. That place held a heap of good memories for me, as well as a whole mound of bad.

"They're meeting Chester Goodwin in Dead Oak," I said.

Rosa started, taken aback. "Goodwin would never leave the safety of Austin."

"No," I said. "He wouldn't. Unless there was something enough to draw him out. Something that he wanted bad enough he'd come get it himself."

Francis said from the doorway. "Something dangerous enough he'd never allow it inside the city for the transfer."

"Or someone," I said. "Francis is the most dangerous hacker this side of Oklahoma, and Chester would never let him set foot in Austin, not even to watch him die. That's Jones's plan."

Rosa said, "If Goodwin's there, we can get to him. That weasel is the driving force behind the oppression of the outlands, ever since he inherited the company. If we kill him—"

"We stop the war," Francis finished, not taking his eyes off me. "But if he gets the virus—"

"The war's over and we lose," I said. I drew a deep breath of air still thick with the fried meat Legs had made for supper. "It's not worth messing with it. We stop the virus and get out."

Reginald spoke up. "If you can blow up the train—"

I scratched the stubble on my chin. "Bombing the train is the easiest approach."

"Shit," Rosa said. She slid a few stars to Legs, who grinned like an idiot.

"Smart," Francis said. "Efficient. Whole lot of folks will die."

"Train is full of Jones's men." I thought of Quin, and the hope she brought out into the world. I'd promised on my honor a long time ago that I wouldn't kill anyone who I wasn't sure had it in for me. Casket Jones and his men would die if we blew up that train. They weren't innocent by any means, but we'd be cowards to let them go out that way.

"We're not going to take the easy way out," I said. "We need to board that train."

Legs scowled and slid the coins back toward a smug Rosa.

"We need to board the train, get the samples, and verify that they're destroyed."

"What if you can't find them all?" Reginald asked.

"Then we keep looking."

Rosa stood, casting one last sorry glance at my hand. "Fine. Come on, Francis. You can help me prep the weapons." She left without another word, drawing Francis with her. She shot me a look as they left. This was meant as a chance for me to brief the others about Francis.

Francis's docility unnerved me more than a little bit. He'd been compliant and helpful the whole time we'd been back, and hadn't given Legs any trouble at all. Every time his cold eyes turned in my direction, a shiver went down my spine. This guy had killed so many. Hell, killing was the least of his crimes.

Yet, there he was, helping us do the right thing. And there I was, letting him help. It didn't feel right in my gut, but I couldn't figure a way to solve the problem that didn't involve a whole lot more violence than I was capable of dishing out.

"That man's dangerous," I said after a long pause. "More dangerous than any of you can know. We need him for this, but I got an itch in the back of my brain tells me that he somehow designed it that way."

"You think he's behind all this?" Trish asked.

"I think he's behind everything, but I can't rightly figure a way to stop him."

Legs stayed behind, shaking his head. "It's more than I wanted to get involved in, old man."

"It's profit," I said. "Fun and games. Right?"

He sighed. "I don't know. Fun isn't what it used to be, you know?"

I looked at him a long time, trying to figure out what hidden layers this man had. Previously, I'd hardly figured he had any layers at all. He'd been a pain in my ass and a career criminal, but not a particularly competent one.

"Rosa and I want kids," Legs finally said. "But how the hell can we raise kids in a place like this?"

"People try anyway." I clenched my fist again. It didn't hurt as much as the first time, but all the joints felt like they were full of sand. "Sometimes they even succeed."

"Yeah," he said, his voice sounding far off. "I wonder if it's even worth it."

"You've got a good spot here," I said. "Acres of land, a clean enough river, and freedom far as the eye can see. If there were any place to raise a family, it'd be here."

"Can you imagine a kid looking up to me, Sheriff?" He gestured at his body. All the flesh he had left was tattooed and scarred. "Can you imagine me telling my kid to stay out of trouble?"

"Kids'll respect your experience."

He shook his head. "I don't know."

I clapped the man on the shoulder on my way to the bedroom. "You'll make as fine a father as you can make, Legs," I said. "Same as anyone else who makes the attempt."

"That's what I'm afraid of."

With that I wandered out to let myself drift into a fitful sleep under the stars. Hours passed in dreams of war. Fights I've fought through all the years caught up with me in sleep, as they'd always done. They scraped at my nerves and prodded at my skull. I'd wake up early to prep for another day.

Another day, another fight. Story of my life.

12

———

Morning came about as fast as morning comes when it's not welcome. Trish nudged me awake with the toe of her boot before the sun had anything like the idea of coming up, and by the time I sat my tired bones up, she was gone. I still wore Legs's bison skull shirt, and I expected it'd be good enough for a few more days. After a moment to stretch my old, aching joints, I slid on my boots and duster. Put on my hat.

Same as any morning.

A quiet rumble thumped at my chest like a second heartbeat pounding in a slow, undulating rhythm. It felt familiar, like the warm sensation of sitting next to a friend at the bar. Near the house, Rosa worked on her van with Quin. The kid already had her shotgun slung across her back, and she wore the knitted poncho she'd worn on our way out of her village. She looked so damn young. Legs hauled supplies from the house, and Trish… Where was Trish?

I motioned Quin over to me, and she practically bounced as she came.

"You're with me," I said.

She pumped a fist.

"We're in back," I told her. "Last car on the train. Get in. Find the seven cases. Place the charges. Then get out." The back would be the safest part of the job. "We won't blow anything up unless we can't find all seven." I tipped my chin at her shotgun. "If it goes well, you won't need that at all."

The rumble intensified, followed by the roar of a solid-state booster.

"What did you and Trish ride from town?" I asked Quin. "Did she have her cruiser?"

Then, as if in answer to my question, my old skidder descended from the sky with a crack-snap of power and a wave of blistering heat. Soon as it touched the earth, Trish hopped off and dusted herself off.

"Where did you get that?" I asked.

"Picked it up a while back."

When I'd fled Dead Oak, I had sent that skidder flying off into the wastelands, sure that it would crash and burn when its fuel got low. It wouldn't have done me much good anymore, but I can't say I didn't miss it. It was a beast of a flying motorcycle, long and meaty where it counts. It floated with proper antigrav, but the bulk of it was the twin boosters, which could pound the bike forward with solid-fuel rockets. Trish had kept it well maintained, and there were even a few shiny new parts among the amalgamation of metalhead inventions.

Trish slapped me on the back. "It's all yours, old man. I'm riding with Sunset."

"I'm surprised you kept it."

"It always pays to make a strong entrance," she said. "This thing became a signature for the Dead Oak sheriff, and folks started to respect it."

Quin ran a hand along the seat. "This is fantastic," she said. "How fast does it go?"

I smiled despite my best efforts. "All the way fast, kid. All the way."

Sunset's own skidder lit up the night like a bonfire. It was the same as we'd seen before, except for an enormous claw mark across the front of the sidecar. Scars from their bear encounter, no doubt. She grinned at me.

"Head for car seven," I told her. "It had cargo and might have a case or two." It was also next to the car with the strange device they were building.

Sunset winked at Trish and I'll be damned if the corner of Trish's mouth didn't twitch up with a smile.

"Legs and Rosa will take the one farther up, since they have better shielding." I crossed the lawn to where Legs and Rosa fit extra armor plates onto her massive van. "Grab and go. Plant charges on your way out, but don't take risks to do it. Detonation's only a backup plan if we fail to find all the cases. Remember, you don't have to shoot to kill. Just brush them back long enough to get a look inside."

Rosa hefted a demo pack and handed it to me. "It'll shear right through metal if you set it up right. Drop it and hit this switch to arm it. That's it."

"Then get out," I said.

"Then get out." She reached into the back of her van and pulled out a gangly-looking black metal device. It looked like an armband crossed with a firehose. "Try this," she said.

I took the device and slipped it over my human hand. It didn't fit well, but I figured out how to tighten the straps in place. The whole thing felt unnatural, but there was a trigger in an awkward place that would let me fire—what?

"It's a needler," Rosa said. "I don't have any black metal needles for it, so you're flinging aluminum."

Aluminum wouldn't have much penetration, but needlers launched the little slivers of metal fast enough it didn't much matter what they were made of. I could tell by the design it wouldn't have much kick, and that'd be better for my still-sore hand. When I slid the device over my hand, it touched the still-open wound. Pain cascaded up my arm. I handed the weapon back.

"I'll pass," I said. "I'm hoping not to need it."

Trish pressed her lips together. "Have you ever not needed a gun to solve a problem, J.D.?"

"Maybe there won't be any problems."

I got back to my skidder and sat on it for a good long time while the others prepped for the attack. The black night sky slowly drifted toward gray, with a hint of color considering its options down in the eastern sky. Sitting on that skidder in the first hints of dawn felt comfortable, but I was wrong about it feeling like a friend. This wasn't a horse that had a give-and-take of real emotion. This was raw power and the freedom of the whole sky. Riding that skidder was something closer to religion.

Quin slid on behind me, and I felt her tension as I fired up the thrusters. Blue flames belched out, scorching the dry earth.

"Wow," she said.

That pretty much covered it.

I gave a whistle and shouted, "Gather up."

The others set down what they were doing and came over. A cool breeze that smelled of mesquite tugged at my coat. Reginald came from the house, and even Francis's eyes stopped flashing with their violet light—as good an indication that I had his attention as a person could expect.

"Now, I know you all have your differences," I said, paying special attention to Rosa and Trish's stiff reactions. "I'm not asking you all to be friends, but this job is going to take cooperation and it's going to take trust. We're riding out to take down Casket Jones, one of Texas's toughest. If that's going to happen, there can't be any doubt about whether or not we've got each other's backs."

Each one of them gave me an affirmative nod. I believed almost half of them. "Now, you all know your parts. We've got limited supplies and that train is well defended. We ride with the rising sun at our backs, and if we're fast it'll all be done in the next hour."

"Back in time for breakfast," Legs said.

Rosa elbowed him. "You already had breakfast, asshole."

"Second breakfast."

"Reggie," I said to the scientist, "anything else we need to know?"

He swallowed and took a step back. "Seems like it'd be easier to blow up the train without trying to board."

"All the same," I said, "I'd like to verify all the crates."

Rosa rolled her eyes. "Making our job harder."

"Even if it makes our job harder."

Reginald said, "You'll need to find the six cases, then, but don't open them."

"Seven," I said.

He nodded, arms crossed over his belly. "Yeah. Seven."

I chuckled at his reaction. "You realize you're the only one here who's not going to get shot at in the next hour, right?"

His eyes flicked too Francis. "I don't want to think about what happens if this gets out."

"Lot of people will die?"

"Yeah. Something like that."

Trish stepped forward. "We'll make sure that doesn't happen, Reginald." She shot a look at Sunset. "We'll all make sure." I wondered what might have passed between the two of them that Trish was able to pressure the bounty hunter to worry about more than her bounty. Sunset, however, gave no visible reaction.

"Well, they spread the weaponized crates throughout the train," Reginald said. He pointed at several cars. "You shouldn't need to check these three near the back. I overheard them saying there was a spill of some sort, and nobody was allowed in those."

I nodded. "I never saw those when I was on the train. I came in around here." I pointed at the train that I'd entered. "There was some kind of device they were working on in this car."

Reginald tensed. "It was something for Casket Jones. Something medical."

It didn't do us much good to think about what treatments someone like Casket Jones was willing to consider for his condition. All that mattered was that they probably wouldn't store the bioweapon there.

"Anything else?" I asked.

Reginald took a step back. "No, that's it."

"Then, let's fly," I said. I kicked my skidder high into the sky, using a blast of blue flame to launch up into the cold dawn air. Quin whooped, clinging close to my back as we rose high into the brightening sky. "Hang on, kid," I said. "This next part's going to get rough."

"Don't I know it," she said.

Below, Rosa's van and Sunset's skidder launched into the air after us.

Quin and I blasted through the sky, sun at our heels. Sunset followed, with Trish riding in her sidecar. Rosa and Legs lagged back, their van more visible in the lightening sky. Francis rode in the back of their vehicle, ready with whatever tech gizmos he thought might help. We raced the orange sunrise, that blazing flame of the sun's first light nipping at our backs the whole way. Those first rays of light would interfere with the train's ability to see us coming. It'd screw with their sensors and blind their watchmen. If we were lucky, they wouldn't even be aware we were coming.

They weren't aware, but for a different reason.

The train wasn't there.

13

———

"Dammit," I said, fumbling with my comm so the rest of the team could properly hear the string of curses I was fixing to unleash. "Legs, I thought you said they were still here."

"They just left," Rosa said. Far behind me, her van launched higher into the sky. "I see them, not far away."

"We should meet them in Dead Oak," Trish said. "If we go forward now, we won't have the sun."

For the stretch of a long breath, I could sense the tension in the air between Rosa and Trish. It came through the silent radio like the hiss of a bobcat. Rosa's van swung, pivoting downward toward us in an angled maneuver just three hairs shy of aggressive. Quin squeezed tight behind me, her strong hands gripping handfuls of my duster.

"We keep at it," I said.

"J.D." Trish's voice was hard, the way it got when she was on the hunt. "We lost our advantage. It's time to call it off."

"I agree," Sunset said.

"Fuck," said Rosa. "Just because we lost a little advantage?"

"Our only advantage," said Trish.

Legs said, "Maybe we should—" His voice cut out sharply.

"Legs agrees with me," Rosa said. "Now hurry before that train's going too fast."

"Rosa's right," I said. When Trish tried to respond, I cut her off. "She's right, Sheriff. This happens now or we risk losing them."

With that, I dropped hard a hundred meters and pounded on the thrust. I didn't look back to see if the others followed, but Quin let out a shriek—first of fear, then of joy. It almost reminded me of the better days of my own youth.

Almost.

We caught up to the train as it accelerated into the bottom of a long canyon. Red rock climbed up around us as we flew low and fast along the tracks. The train hadn't hit full speed—not even close. We'd have to get in and get the job done before it outstripped the sheer power of our little vehicles. I might have the raw thrust to get up as fast as the train, but my face wasn't anywhere near as aerodynamic. Things got real painful at those speeds.

The wind smelled of burnt earth and freedom, just as Texas always did in the summer. It scoured our faces with heat and dust. Fast as we were moving, the air became abrasive as any lava rock. I tucked my head down so the bulk of it slid past, and Quin hugged close behind me to stay safe.

The first turret popped up seconds after we rounded the long bend and came within sight of the train. So much for surprise. Somewhere behind us, a thunderous rattle shook the cavern walls and the turret dissolved in a haze of sparks. Two more took its place.

I pounded the thrust, taking the low, fast route while Sunset covered us. The turrets returned her fire, and the air above us grew thick with hot metal. Twenty meters and we'd hit the train. Ten.

Five.

Another turret extended from the rear of the train, too close to avoid. I swung the bike around and shouted, "Hit it, Quin!"

Quin drew her shotgun in one smooth movement, gripping my coat with her other hand. She leveled it at the turret from five meters away. The bike bucked. She fired.

Missed.

A bloom of hot slag flashed on the plating next to the turret. I swore and launched us to one side.

Not fast enough. Bullets raked across the side of the bike, thudding into the right thruster. Something hissed fierce as we spun hard to the side. Quin took another shot, this time with worse odds.

She hit. The turret shriveled under a molten-hot slug.

Wrestling for control of the bike, I swung us in a wide loop around the back of the train. We slung along the side, careful to avoid another turret while Sunset dealt with it. She had the most tricked-out bike I'd ever seen and having Trish in the sidecar made the pair about as deadly as anything I'd ever encountered in the desert.

Having dealt with the turrets, Sunset and Rosa rocketed over us in their respective vehicles.

"Get ahead," I said. "Hit 'em quick and let's get out of here."

I fired a grapple from the front of the bike, latching hard onto the rear of the train. It was still speeding up, and with the bike anchored, we were pulled ever faster. This was a hell of a lot harder than boarding a stopped train, and every jolt that ran through the taut cable sent shivers of fear down my spine.

"I'll slow the train," Francis said over the line.

"Hell of a lot of good that did the other day," I muttered.

"I had just woken up." He didn't sound annoyed at my comment. He didn't sound much of anything. It seemed when he flexed that computer in his head he lost any remaining shreds of humanity he had left. I was talking to a robot.

The back of the train was a tapered design—no doubt for

aerodynamics—but still had a ledge and a door that could slide open to allow entrance. No doubt it was sealed when the train moved. Nobody would ever want to step outside for a smoke when this train was moving as fast as it moved. Locked didn't bother me much. I jumped from the bike to the ledge and shot a look back at Quin to make sure she was covering me.

With a grunt, I jammed the three fingers of my metal hand into the door and wrenched it clean off. I ducked to the side, and Quin fired two shots into the hall. When she gave me an all-clear, I ducked into the train and waved her forward.

My ears popped from the drop in pressure. The hole in the back of the train sucked air out of the confined space, making the dark, cluttered car feel like a nosebleed of a near-space cargo hauler. Boxes like the ones I'd spilled over the landscape filled the space—but not the crates we were looking for.

"Getting some trouble up here," said Rosa. "Shit." Her feed filled with the chatter of gunfire. "No, never mind. We're fine."

"What the hell?" Trish said. "Some kinda machine up here, but no crates."

She had found the device the men in black had been setting up. No time to deal with it now. "Set a bomb in there if you get a chance."

The bomb pack didn't need to be in any particular place, so long as it was inside the train car it was meant to slag. It might take out the adjacent cars, but if Rosa had balanced it right, it was a drop-and-go job. I primed the pack and stashed it behind the first row of tied-down cargo.

"Bomb's set," I said. "No crates back here."

Just then, Quin dropped down next to me in the car. She had a fiery panic in her eyes.

"What is it?"

She tackled me hard. Bullets riddled the cargo, punching deep black holes in the shielded luggage.

"Taking fire from behind!" I shouted into the channel.

Quin clutched her shotgun in two hands. I read the terror in her eyes and knew she wouldn't be any good. Hazarding a glance out the ruined door earned me another barrage of bullets and an idea of what we were facing.

Rosa's voice crackled over the line. "Three crates up here—goddamnit!" The feed descended into a chaos of gunfire.

Casket Jones rode an open-top cruiser modified with black chrome thrust plates and a bristling array of weapons. On a good day, he'd be a force to be reckoned with, and I hadn't had a good day in a long damn time.

His voice came over the train's internal PA. "Couldn't leave enough alone, could you, J.D.? Least you could do is let us win the war for you."

"You're not winning the war, Jones," I growled. "You're handing the enemy the weapons to kill us all."

His laugh was mocking and harsh. "Us? You count yourself among us now? I thought you'd risen above the common people of Texas. Too good to fight our wars."

The boxes in the center of the floor were clipped down. With a swipe I broke the clip off and shoved the whole pallet to block the door. We needed time, and Casket Jones wasn't likely to give it to us.

"Francis," I said through the feed. "You got control of that train yet?"

"Partially."

"Speed us up. Push it as fast as it'll go."

"You won't be able to escape."

"We need to lose, Jones."

The train lurched forward, acceleration pressing the crates harder against the rear door.

"Ah fuck," cried Legs over the line. "What are you doing?"

"He's fine," Rosa said.

"We're set," said Trish. "Two crates. You want us to take a shot at Jones on our way out?"

"No," I said. "We'll handle him."

Pulling Quin with, I crossed to the far end of the car. The door opened, and we ducked through to the space between cars. If things got too ugly, Casket Jones could start hitting hard, and we didn't want to be anywhere close.

I put a hand on Quin's shoulder. "You okay?"

She nodded, swallowing the panic that was so obviously ready to consume her.

"All we gotta do is escape." Into the channel, I said, "Legs, you ready?"

"Yeah," he said with obvious strain in his voice. "We're good to go."

The train rattled under our feet, strain evident in the whine of the antigrav and stabilizers.

"Go then, but stay close. I'm going to find a way up."

"Up?" Quin asked. "Are you sure?"

"Trains like these always have ways to access the roof. We'll crawl across the top to get back to the skidder."

Trish's voice came over the line. "J.D., you're an idiot. The wind'll take your face off."

Shit. "Hold on," I said. "I'll come up with something."

"We still need two more crates," she said.

"Then let's find them."

Reginald had warned us not to try to search the whole train, but we had time. Part of me wondered what was spilled in those cars near the back. That was one car away from where we stood. Did I dare go in?

Damn right I dared.

I motioned for Quin to stand to the side. Opening the door, I edged my way in, waiting for my eyes to adjust. The smell that hit me was a wave of stale sweat and piss. Air thick with flies and reeking of shit rolled into the space between cars. Quin gagged.

The car was dark, and shadows of movement told me we

weren't alone. I stepped forward, careful not to make too much noise. There still might be someone dangerous in there, but every instinct in my gut told me the only people there were poor and destitute. Prisoners maybe. Or slaves.

Quin found a switch for the lights and powered it up. The smell hadn't hindered me, but the sight nearly made me sick. People—human beings—were crammed into cages like dogs. Their filthy flesh was pressed against the metal bars of locked cages. Dozens of them stared at me with the whites of their eyes showing in the bright, harsh light.

"Dammit," I said through the channel. "Goddamnit. We need to call it off."

"What?" Trish said.

I tested the lock on the nearest cage. It wouldn't budge. "Legs, I thought you said they didn't collect anyone while they were stopped."

"They didn't!" Legs's voice crackled with static.

Rosa's voice came through strong. "The train's losing Jones."

"Call what off, J.D.?" Trish said.

"All of it. Don't blow the charges. There are people on this train. Dozens of them."

A wave of impact pulsed through the train. I didn't know if it was a bomb or just the trains systems failing. Either way, it wasn't good.

I looked to Quin. She stared wide-eyed at the people in their cages. Not a damn one of them spoke, and by the wild looks in their eyes, they weren't likely to be chatting anytime soon. I strolled through the room, floor rattling under my feet.

"Francis," I said. "Slow the train. Not so much that Jones can catch up, but enough we won't crash."

The train immediately slowed, and Quin stumbled into me.

"Everyone, get back to the train. Now."

"What?" Rosa said. "What the hell for?"

"Things have changed," I said. Casket Jones was trafficking

in human beings. No matter if they were prisoners of war, slaves for an army, or just human beings to experiment on, they were people. We needed to get them to safety, and the original plan of bombing and running wasn't going to get it done. "Get back. This is our damn train now."

14

"Well where the hell did they come from?" My voice rumbled just shy of a yell, and Legs winced at every word.

"I told you," he said. "We had eyes on all the locals. They didn't pick these folks up when they stopped."

Trish cut me off before anger boiled out again. "He's right." She sniffed the air. "You smell that?"

"What?" All I smelled was the sour stink people got before they gave up all hope. Then it clicked. "How long have you people been here?" I asked.

Not a damn one of them responded. They didn't even bother looking up at me—not even a glance. As the train sped across the Texan landscape, they stood there like cattle awaiting slaughter. Maybe that's what they were.

"Get Reginald on the line," I said. "He knows something he's not telling you."

"I've tried." Trish gripped the bar of one of the cages, her artificial muscles flexing their furious strength. I'd never seen her so frustrated. Every attempt to open the cages had failed.

Even my big metal arm couldn't tear these bars free. "We don't even know if these people are infected."

But something was wrong with them. They looked like common folk: tan-skinned farmers and brown-skinned bankers. Young and old stood crammed in cages that ran the length of the train car.

"Did we find the crates?"

Trish peered closely at me. "Six total."

"We need to talk to Reggie, goddamnit," I said, almost to myself.

"Can't get him, boss," Legs said from the other end of the train car. "Francis tried."

"Have you tried?"

Legs shook his head.

"Try. And have Rosa try too. I don't trust Francis."

"I can hear you, you know," Francis said over the train's speakers.

"I fucking know you can. Something's rotten out here and I'd like to know what. How long till we get to Dead Oak?"

Trish's eyes flashed with the data. "Not much longer."

"We're stopping there," I said. "We need to get these people to safety." I tried the lock again, but it resisted. Somebody really wanted these people locked up.

Rosa said, "You want us to destroy the crates?"

"Yeah," I said. "When we get stopped, stick them in a hole and use one of those bombs. Trish, make sure that happens."

Dead Oak was always a small town situated at the ass end of nowhere. It was far enough from everything to be something, but close enough to Austin to be nothing. Dead Oak had the unfortunate situation of being in the middle of the worst when anything bad hit. Its domed buildings withstood every storm, but its people never thrived. I'd once dragged justice kicking and screaming to this hellhole of a town, but the work I did had been nothing compared to the hardscrabble everyday lives of its citizens.

That's why it was a damn surprise when I stepped off the train in the Dead Oak station to find a bustling little village full of commerce and activity.

I strolled into the center of town under the pulsing flow of flying traffic overhead. The massive dead oak still stood in the central square, its knobby branches clawing at the deep blue sky. Even the tree seemed fuller than it had been when I left, some representation of the thriving town in general.

Or, as I discovered when I got closer, it was full of crows. The whole murder muttered at me as I approached, their evil eyes staring me down like they knew I was their namesake. Maybe some of them wanted their name back. I hadn't bore it very well.

Crows were a symbol of luck to the Hopi, I knew. If that was true, Dead Oak had won its fair share of good fortune while I had been away. Maybe the town could thrive after all.

"I don't know what to do," I said to the crows. "I used to always try to do the right thing, but there don't seem to be all too many right things left."

The crows didn't answer. At the top of the tree, several birds lifted off into the clear blue to circle high above the little town.

"Those folks in the train—slaves, I think—there's something wrong with them. Something broken." I took off my hat and held it in my aching hand. "I'm afraid to move them or set them free. They won't talk. What if they carry the disease that Reginald warned us about?"

Several more crows flew up into the sky. A few saw fit to land on the surrounding buildings. One landed on the sheriff's office and another landed on the tavern. Those were the hard choices, weren't they?

I closed my eyes for a long time, feeling the last rays of the setting sun on my face. It reminded me of Sunset and how hard she'd fought for the cause. Trish had listed a bounty for Jones as soon as she saw the prisoners, but Sunset had fought hard the whole way through. She was good folk, even though she worked a job mostly populated by assholes like Casket Jones. And me.

"I haven't figured out what to do. If we're right, Goodwin is on his way, and I'd bet my hat that Casket Jones is rallying his troops to take back the train. It's an ugly situation all around, and there's no place for us to go. We're going to have a fight." The muscles in my hand gave an involuntary twitch.

Dozens of crows launched into the air. The darkening sky grew thick with them. When all settled, only one remained on the tree. I approached, and it watched me with wary eyes.

My fingers touched the grip of one of my pistols. I'd found my gear on the train, but my hand still ached so much I wasn't sure if I could properly use them. Something about that crow made my mouth taste like bitter ash.

"I fight when I must," I said. "Maybe it'll be the end of me, or maybe I'll win."

"That'd be a first," said Trish behind me.

The last crow called out and took to the sky. It circled three times and then disappeared behind one of the domed buildings.

"I learned a long time ago that you never win a fight. You just lose less hard."

She placed a hand on my shoulder. "There's a lot more to it than winning. The people of this town could use you back."

"There's not a warrant out for me anymore?"

"I'm the sheriff, J.D. There hasn't been a warrant out for you in years. Soon as the heat died down, I took you off the list."

I strolled past the tree and down the street, taking in Dead Oak in all its glory. "Town's done well," I said. There were new domes at the outskirts and several new tenement buildings. Storefronts lined one row of new construction, and the people walking the streets almost looked happy. "You've done well."

"They did well when you were around too."

"Not this well." Something clicked in my head. Why was she trying to downplay this success? My gut made the kind of noise it made when folks were dodging the truth. "The new tracks that go straight to Austin. Dead Oak is getting rich dealing both sides."

"We scrape by as best we can."

A knot of rage twisted in my chest. "You scrape by better than anyone else in the area. Dead Oak trades goods with the enemy and gets fat off the profit." My voice came out louder than intended.

Trish's jaw clenched. "We do what we need. You think we'd deal with Austin if we had a choice? This town dies without them. We need medicine and tech, J.D. They need food."

"Folks have lived without tech in Texas."

She crossed in front of me and jabbed a finger in my chest. "People suffer without tech. Lots of folks—yourself included—depend on it for day-to-day life. You think that arm of yours is any different from what anyone else needs?"

"I didn't ask for this." My voice was small.

"You didn't, and neither did Franny who requires insulin or her son Hank who was born without kidneys." She nodded politely as the two pedestrians strolled by. "Neither did that punk Legs who was injured when his idiot father died trying to mess with explosives so he could rob a bank."

"Was that what happened?" I'd always thought the man had replaced his legs as a voluntary upgrade.

"It's in your own goddamn records, J.D." Her voice pitched to a grating yell. "You were there on the scene after it happened. It's just that his tragedy was so damn common you forgot him."

I gritted my teeth. We were outside the bar, and it was taking all my will not to go in and obliterate myself with whiskey. "None of that," I said. "None of that makes war profiteering okay."

Her fists clenched at her sides. She could kill with those fists. "The commerce happens because I allow it, and it's for the best."

"Is that why you were in Candlestick? So you could make sure the best thing for your people got on board that train? Were you aware there were slaves? Or did it just not matter to you?"

Those fists didn't move, but her glare damn near killed me. After a good long look at me, she stalked off toward the train still parked at the station outside of town.

"Word is Casket Jones is on his way," she called back as she left. "Could use your help defending the train."

"You mean the people," I said under my breath. "You need help defending the people."

A beat-up old truck landed a dozen meters from the tree. Out of it stepped a man I thought I'd never see again: Ben Brown. Francis's older brother. He stood tall and strong, like the rancher he now was, but the artifacts of his youth still stood strong on his flesh. Proud tattoos, some ink, some tech decorated his muscular arms. His hair stood in ragged red spikes.

"Thought I heard you were in town," Ben said without turning to greet me.

A woman stepped out of the other side of the vehicle. She was slender but for a prominent baby bump that forced her to walk back on her heels. Abi had been a fierce girl when last I'd seen her. Now she was a fiercer woman with dark skin and a smile brighter than the sun in the sky.

"Welcome back, J.D.," she said as she opened the back of the truck. A couple of horses, a tall chestnut and a black gelding, stepped out.

I tipped my hat to her. "I found your brother," I said to Ben, feeling the lameness of the words as they came out.

He took the reigns of the chestnut and started checking the straps of the saddle. "You could have come back years ago, J.D."

"Sure," I said.

The gelding grew skittish, but Abi kept it under control with a few soothing words. She walked it in a big circle.

"I'm doing well here," Ben said. "Power's got a good market so the wind farm's in good shape."

"You still raising the best steaks in Texas?"

"Biggest, anyway."

"Same thing."

Wartime was doing well for him. Protected as he was, the ranch could make a killing selling the Austin. The enemy. Hell, he'd probably had cargo meant to go on the train we'd captured. It didn't seem right to bring it up to the man. Ben had always been full of fire, but the man in front of me was a smoldering ember waiting to be put out. He held a hand on the chestnut's flank.

"We could use your gun," I said. "Word is there's a gang on its way."

"I'm married now, old man," he said. "I don't run off no more."

"Never thought I'd see you married."

He grinned a goofy grin at Abi as she circled around back with the skittish gelding. "With a kid on the way. It's something people do still, you know."

"So I've heard. Congratulations." I couldn't think of anything else to say, even though it wasn't a world I'd ever bring a kid into. "I suppose you're out too, then?" I said to Abi.

The scowl she sent me would have been a damn fine one if she hadn't broken down into laughter at the end of it. "Ask me again in a month, J.D."

Ben took her hand in his and gave it a squeeze. "Any who wanted to fight already left town to join a side. You won't find any help in Dead Oak or anywhere close."

"Used to be this was an honorable place," I said, my hackles up. The gelding shied away from me. "Folks fought for what they believed in, even if they believed in stupid things."

Ben tensed, and his horse shook its head. "Is that what this is? Something stupid? Not making a great case, are you?"

"Debate was never my strong suit."

"No, you had guns for that. Well, maybe some of us don't want to live in a place where guns are the solution to everything. Austin's fight isn't with us. It's with up north and the coastlanders. They pay well for what we sell, and at the end of the day, we're as important to them as they are to us."

"And that's why the new tracks run straight through the Brown Ranch?"

"The train runs both ways," he said. "Just because I don't discriminate who I sell to doesn't mean I'm siding with an enemy."

The gelding took a step toward me again, and I managed to get a hand on its neck. Dust came off in clouds, evidence of a hard dry day out in the Texas wastes. I almost felt bad for the horse, but then I remembered that the animal probably had more freedom than most of the people I knew. At least this gelding could run from time to time.

"There were two warrants out for Francis," I said. "Somebody wanted him alive, somebody wanted him dead. Neither one identified who exactly was paying the bounty, but Trish wanted him alive."

Ben gently brushed the chestnut for several long strokes, settling it back down. "There ain't a bounty high enough for what my brother's done."

"People forget," I said. "Forgetting's almost as good as forgiving sometimes."

"And how honorable is that?"

"Not even a little." I drew a deep breath. Ben had always impressed me as a kid, even when he was skirting on the edge of the law. "Look Ben, Francis is still around. He *wants* to be in town and I don't know why. Come help us, maybe you can figure him out."

Ben scoffed. "Figure him out? I never could figure him out. After all he did to those people? Nobody can figure that guy out. He broke when Ma died. There's no getting better."

"You mean when I killed your ma," I said in a low voice. "I know this is all my fault. I could have done so much better by him, and I failed. My honor's in a ruined, bloody mess, and it always has been. All I'm asking is for some help saving some folks from trouble."

Ben set his brush down. He led his chestnut into her stall and locked the gate. "Find help somewhere else," he said, mounting the chestnut. "I got errands to run."

Despite her condition, Abi hoisted herself up onto the gelding. It sidestepped a few times, but within seconds she had it under control.

After that, Ben said nothing. I walked back through town to the train as the sun's final illumination faded from the gray-white sky.

15

———————

I strode alongside the sleek metal monstrosity. How could we defend this thing against the folks coming to take it back? It sure as hell hadn't defended against us very well.

Inside, I walked the whole length of the train. Five cars held prisoners—over a hundred total. Every cage was locked with nearly indestructible black metal, like the stuff that made up my arm. It'd be a hell of a hard thing to bust these people out. What was so special about these passengers? Not a single one of them spoke to me, but a few glanced in my direction as I made my way past. They were a filthy lot, clothed in rags and covered in red dust. Workers of some sort, by the looks of their hands. Miners, farmers.

Blood covered the walls in the cargo car that I'd split open on my first escape from the train. A couple of Jones's men had made their final stand against Legs and Rosa in that thin-walled car, and they'd paid the price for it. They'd managed to close the walls again, but the hundred holes in the metal made a solid case that one needed to carefully select one's cover, especially when up against someone as trigger-happy as Legs.

I found Francis in the fancy car closest to the front. He stood facing forward, away from the door, so he couldn't have seen me come in. He knew I was there anyway.

"You need me to move the train," he said in his flat voice.

Anger boiled in my gut. This wasn't how capturing a bounty was supposed to turn out. The bounty didn't give orders. I drew my weapon, the revolver with the Red Number Five chambered and ready for him. "Who says I want to move the train? Talked to your brother."

In that same flat voice, he said, "You've been into town."

"I want to talk to Francis," I said. "The real Francis, with his whole brain working."

After a long pause, Francis said without inflection, "This is the real Francis, Sheriff. There isn't anything else."

I raised the revolver, pointing it at the back of his head.

"You won't shoot," he said.

"Why not? Because there's no honor in shooting a man in the back? Because there's no challenge in it?"

"No," he said, turning around to focus glowing white eyes on me. "Because it doesn't bring you suffering."

I locked his gaze for a long time, but in the end I looked away. He was right. I lowered my weapon, but I didn't stow it. My fingers ached from the simple effort of holding it.

"You see," he said. "That's the difference between you and me. You choose to suffer every day in everything that you do. You push yourself past pain and you let the sun scour your flesh. You eat terrible food and wallow in the agony of those you've lost." He took a step forward. "I have the strength to choose a different path."

The tension in my neck ached so bad my hand shook, so I holstered my weapon. I couldn't think of any response to him. "Why do we need to move the train?"

He didn't smile, not even in the slightest crease of his sallow flesh. "We're exposed here, and farther ahead there is a hill that this track cuts through."

"The tunnels up by your brother's ranch."

"He hardly considers me his brother."

"Family's harder to shake than that, Francis," I said, but I wondered if it wasn't true. "I'll need you to move the train, but wait for my signal." Some shred of honor in me told me I couldn't kill him. Not unless I absolutely had to in the middle of a furious combat. Even then I'd probably only wound him.

What was it about Francis William Brown that cut so deep to the core of my own suffering? It had been years since that day I'd killed his mother. Hadn't that been a bullet fired in the middle of honorable combat? We're all warriors once we pick up the gun. We're all casualties of our own wars, no matter if we walk away or feed the worms.

"I think you're wrong," I said after it became apparent that Francis wouldn't respond. "There is more to you than what I'm seeing now. I saw that look in your eyes when you came out of that coffin." When he still didn't say anything, I left.

"Hey," Quin said as I stepped out onto the red earth around the middle of the train. She sat atop the train with her shotgun on her lap.

"Hey, kid," I said.

She scowled. It was a scowl to be proud of. Scathing.

"You don't want to be called a kid," I said.

"I screwed up," she said. "I thought I had it all figured out, and then I screwed up when things went bad."

"C'mon," I said, and waited for her to climb down. We walked a short distance to a place where the remains of an old fence crossed an empty field. The night air smelled of a silence full of danger. It made my skin prickle. "You're a football player," I said eventually. "And a damn fine one."

She slung her shotgun across her back. "I almost got us killed."

"No, *I* almost got us killed." I drew my second revolver, the one with standard bullets. "But the thing you need to realize is that things always fall apart. Not one damn plan has ever gone off without a hitch."

"Sounds like you aren't very good at making plans."

"And football players aren't very good at changing on the fly. In the real world, you don't get a huddle. When the enemy's in your face or at your back, you move fast and plan without thinking."

"That sounds a lot like not planning at all."

I shook my head. "Going without a plan will get you killed for sure." I handed the gun to her. "Look," I said, "this is your new backup plan. It's too big for you to fire properly, and it's only got five bullets."

She looked at the weapon in her hands, hefting it. "It's huge."

"If you ever need it, huge is going to be an advantage. It'll kick like a mule, but it'll punch holes in skulls."

Quin shuddered. "This… doesn't help at all, J.D."

I unclipped my holster belt for that weapon and handed it to her. "No," I said, "but I was tired of carrying around a revolver I couldn't properly use. This way you'll know you've got a backup plan."

She tightened the belt around her waist and holstered the revolver. It looked good on her, if a little large. The grip sat right on her hip where it was easy for her to draw quickly.

"Panic happens when there's no backup plan. If the plan you're executing doesn't have any way out, it's easy to fall to mistakes. When you go in with options, you have choices, and then all you gotta do is follow your instinct." I put a hand on her shoulder. "You've got good instincts, kid. Trust them."

Quin didn't look convinced.

"Well," I said to Quin. "This is your chance to back down. Stay in town, and I'll buy you a drink at the tavern afterwards."

She sucked her teeth for a good ten seconds. "My gut tells

me this is tied to something bigger, and I need to figure out what. Plus, I'm pretty sure you'll keep me safe."

"Huh," I said on our way back to the train. "Maybe your instincts aren't so good after all."

16

"This is a huddle," Quin said. "You said there wouldn't be any huddles."

Trish stepped forward. "Jones and his gang have been spotted on approach. They're moving in fast, and they'll be here soon. We can only assume they plan to take the train back."

"I said there *might* not be time for a huddle." I looked at each of them in turn: Quin, Trish, Sunset, Francis, Legs, and Rosa. "But this is a huddle. Where are we on defenses."

Legs said, "Rosa and I got one of the rear turrets up."

"Those were worthless against us," I said.

Rosa nodded in Francis's direction. "He's able to control it directly, so it'll make better targeting decisions."

"All right," I said. "Also, don't accelerate as hard as you can. This whole train vibrates when you do that and it'll throw off our aim."

Francis gave an almost imperceptible nod as a response. He didn't meet my gaze.

"Sunset, your vehicle is our biggest weapon, but I'd like to keep it inside. There's no telling what they have coming, and I don't want you overwhelmed."

Sunset scowled. "When am I getting a shot at Casket?"

"Soon enough," Trish said. "I've put out the bounty on him. Two thousand stars, since he's wanted for trafficking humans."

"Isn't that what we're doing now?" Quin asked. "I mean, with the people?"

"No," I said. "We're relocating them until we can figure out how to get one of them to talk and possibly get them out of their cages. I'd sure like to have a chat with Reginald about that."

"He's still incognito," Rosa said. "I had someone stop by the house, and he's not there anymore."

Shit. "Until we figure out whether or not those prisoners are infected, it's our duty to protect them from anyone who would do them harm."

"Our duty?" Trish asked with a crooked smile on her face. "Are you deputizing us, Sheriff?"

I ground my teeth.

"He's right," she said, her tone becoming serious. "You can all consider yourselves deputized."

Legs snorted a laugh.

"Even you two." Trish gave Legs and Rosa a hard look.

"We need to figure out what the deal is with the prisoners," I said to Rosa. "Where they came from, where they're headed, and why they won't talk." The more I thought about it, the more it bothered me.

Rosa put her hands on her hips. "What do you want me to do about it?"

"Stay with me. Sunset can fire out the back, and Legs, Trish, and Quin should cover whichever side the enemy comes from hardest. "We'd like Jones's gang to try to board from the back, if possible, since that'll give us a better single point of defense."

"How do we do that?"

"We get to the tunnel," I said. "As fast as possible."

"Without accelerating hard," Francis said.

"Yup."

Quin shook her head. "This is a great plan."

Sunset nodded and left for the back of the train. The others spread out, each manning a separate car to spread out the defense. I wished to hell I had more men to get this job done. Even if we'd only had Ben's gun we'd have been in better shape.

"Let's move," I said to Francis.

The train jolted forward, hard at first, then moving into a steady acceleration. Francis returned to the main cabin, not because of the comfort available there—he never bothered sitting—but probably because the room gave him the fastest access to the train's main computers. The doors between there and the cargo car were still torn from their hinges, a testament to the battle I'd fought there.

Rosa and I moved to the first train with prisoners, back behind the passenger cars.

"What's the deal, old man?" Rosa asked. "We should get out there and fight, not piss around in here."

"Something about this smells sour." I turned to her, feeling the pressure of dozens of empty eyes on us. "I think someone's going to double-cross us."

She tensed. "Who?"

"I don't know yet. Could be Sunset. Trish has been acting funny, but I tend to trust her to do the right thing."

"Legs?"

"I have not once ever trusted Legs, and it's always turned out to be a good policy."

She nodded, understanding. Along one side of the car, the row of prisoners pressed against the bars of the cage. A man with a bushy beard and tattoo on his bald head smiled through gapped teeth.

"And there's Francis. Something doesn't fit here, like he's fixin' to spring something on us last second." Outside, the first gunshots sounded like rolling thunder, and tension ran like a rabid coyote up my spine. "I need your help keeping an eye on them."

"All of them?" Rosa squeezed my elbow. "J.D., you're right to not trust anyone, but what do you think we can do?"

"Keep an ear to the ground. If you hear or see anything suspicious, let me know."

She threw her hands up. "Great. I'll do that."

The narrow windows on the left side of the train lit up as if it were broad daylight. The prisoners on that side all flinched and cowered, and a second later, the whole train shook. I shot a look at Rosa, but she didn't seem bothered. She was busy peering at the big bearded man with the bald head.

"Why are you trusting me?" Rosa asked without taking her eyes off the man.

I wanted to tell her that I didn't trust anyone. Folks who had endured a hard life like hers hardly needed explanation of paranoia, but that's not the message I wanted to send. "I know Legs wants kids," I said. "Do you?"

That shocked her attention back to me. She pointed a finger at my chest. "It's none of your business."

"I trust a person looking for a future a whole lot more than someone with none," I said. "And you'd do a lot worse than Legs, if he's really as ready to settle as he sounds."

"But you still don't trust Legs?"

"No. That guy's an ass."

"Where do you want me?" she asked, drawing her gun.

"Left side, forward cargo car. Where we had the huddle. I'll take the next cargo car back. The first one with no prisoners."

She stalked away without another word. I made my way back a couple cars to the cargo car I'd scoped out earlier. A gaping hole howled in the increasing wind—testament to the firepower Sunset had unleashed earlier. I took up a position where a crate gave me the illusion of cover and hazarded a peek outside.

The Texas night spread out before me. High above, the roof of the world was lit by a trillion stars, held in solid contrast to the Lone Star of Texas below. Shadowed giants of great, black windmills stood sentry among the twisted live oaks of the desert's edge. Far away, on the other side of the vast horizon, Austin churned like a stirred anthill, and little towns fought against her oppressive influence. Here, the world was quiet but for one minor thing.

Us.

Shots rang out through the vast, quiet night.

Bullets pierced the thin train walls, punching at sharp angles to make oval shapes of stark black against the shining metal. I ducked back, behind the crates. Walls would obscure me, but the folks outside shot bullets big enough to make jokes out of thin steel and corpses out of armored men.

The shooter was close. From cover, I listened to the whistling wind. The train was fast, but nowhere near its top speed. With so many ruined aerodynamics, Francis would have been a fool to move at half the train's potential, and Francis was no fool.

The noise shifted, covering the rush of wind with a thump-thump of a straining gravity drive. The shooter must be close. The noise of the wind shifted again.

I leapt over the crates and shot a metal arm out the hole, grabbing hard at whatever I could get. My fingers clamped onto a skidder, flying close to the train. Too close. I slammed the slender bike into the side of the train, and it spiraled off to explode against the rocky earth.

But its rider wasn't on it.

Two feet swung down from above, kicking me hard in the chest. In the blackness of the dark train car, the man was a shadow of quicksilver and pain. He punched hard at my face— glancing blows deflected by my quick reflex.

I lashed out at him and stumbled back, instinct telling me to make space. Space was the last thing I wanted. Soon as I was a meter away, I heard the telltale sound of the slide action on a large pistol.

Shit.

Muzzle flash lit the car like a lightning strike as I dove to the side. A tug at my coat meant he'd barely missed, and when I landed, pain shot up my bad hand. I scrambled forward, boots making too much noise to ever sneak away. More shots, but wild this time. He was blinded by his weapon's phosphorescent blaze.

That same blaze told me exactly where to do business. With my metal arm, I lifted one crate and threw it hard as I could. I heard a grunt of surprise and the crack of bones. I threw another crate his way, but it flew wide.

"You're on the wrong side," he said through obvious pain.

I stood in the train, wind howling at the gaping hole like a coyote crying in the night. His words hung in the air like a sheet drying in the breeze. Thing is, he might be right. I'd never much had any luck picking sides. Until I figured out what was going on, there weren't any sides except protecting those people.

I said, "What—"

He fired, and the bullet passed close enough to my ear that I heard its screaming death over the wail of the wind. It tugged at the brim of my hat. I lunged forward and jabbed hard with the pointed fingers of my metal hand, and his skull popped like a watermelon.

His gun clattered to the floor.

"Francis," I said through the comm. "How far are we from the ravine?"

"Three minutes."

Damn. Too long. I shoved crates up against the wall, hoping to dissuade any other boarders. Of course, it wouldn't really slow them down if they were determined, but if Sunset did her job well, she'd have sent out the message loud and clear. The rear of the train was the easiest place to board, and once they figured that out, they'd focus on it.

Hopefully.

Back in forward cargo, I found Rosa fighting off boarders of her own. Only, she fought three of them and she did it with style. Moonlight shone through the gaping hole in the cargo wall.

I stepped into the car as she kicked a tall man off the train. He hit the ground and rolled, becoming a tangled mess and a smear across the rocky Texan landscape. A short guy with a tightly trimmed beard dove for a gun, which was on the floor in the corner. Rosa flicked a knife, pinning his hand to the wall.

He screamed and yanked the blade out, blood welling up from the wound. The last combatant—a woman with fists like jackhammers—closed the distance to Rosa, tackling her with overwhelming force.

Rosa rolled and tucked, throwing the woman against the far wall. The man picked up his gun in his left hand.

But before I could blink, Rosa crossed the car and slashed his neck with a wicked hunting knife. Dark blood welled up and he toppled. She swiped her throwing knife up from where the man dropped it and flicked it, burying it in the woman's eye.

She turned and gave me a shrug. I picked the guy up and tossed him out the hole. Then I did the same with the woman. No need to keep them around.

"Francis," I said.

"It's been twenty-seven seconds since I told you three minutes." Was that a hint of annoyance?

"We're slowing down," I said.

"Stopping is much easier if we slow down first."

Rosa smirked. "He has a point."

I said, "Sometimes I think he has more of a sense of humor than he lets on." I thought about it for a minute. "Twisted sense of humor, though."

Shooting a look outside, I saw that there weren't any more flyers on the way in. They must be at the back of the train or too high above for me to see. I clenched my fist, feeling the raw ache in the bones. Damn. I wished I could properly fire a weapon almost as much as I wished there wasn't a need to fire one.

On the floor in the corner sat the man's pistol, a snubnosed revolver with small-caliber bullets. I picked it up and checked it over. It'd do in a pinch. Only a fool fires another man's weapon, but what the hell, right? The kick couldn't be much, and it wouldn't poke through armor or most skin augments, but it'd get someone's attention just fine. I checked the cylinder. Seven bullets.

Rosa and I made our way to the back of the train. We passed Quin and Trish, leaving them to watch their posts. They'd held their ground well, keeping anyone from getting anywhere close to their parts of the train. Legs appeared from nowhere and startled the bejesus out of me, but he tucked right in and followed.

As we approached the end of the train, I heard gunshots over the howling rush of wind. Hurrying, I came to the second to last train, where Sunset crouched behind cover clutching a bloody shoulder. In the final car, half a dozen of boarders held out, and I could see through the narrow passage Casket Jones's convertible floated in sync behind the slowing train.

"Jones!" I shouted. "Turn yourself over, son. It's done."

Jones's fellas stopped shooting, and I waved Sunset back. Rosa lay her down to take a look at her shoulder. Casket Jones himself stepped up out of his vehicle, walked across the hood of his own car, and stepped into the train.

"I won't let you make this deal, J.D."

What the hell deal was he talking about? "These people aren't mine any more than they're yours."

"The people. Reginald's subjects used to perfect the same thing he used to infect me."

"So he knew about them."

"They're his, with all the healing his virus gives me plus a virally delivered lobotomy." He grinned. "Keeps them obedient."

"If he had it working, why weaponize that?"

"Weaponize? He was making doses that wouldn't lobotomize the subjects."

"For Goodwin."

A smile twisted his tumors. His fingers twitched near the action of his red revolver. "You always struck me as a good man," he said. "Why care about someone like Chester Goodwin?"

I stepped out of cover and faced the man. Only a few meters separated us, and I kept my fingers close to my weapon just as he did his. There was no hope at all of my outdrawing him, but the situation called for a little bravado, and that was something I had to spare. "I know as well as anyone that Goodwin's a crook."

His eyes narrowed and he studied me. "Not one good thing ever came out of Austin. Not their money, not their power, not their tech. Not their goddamn biomods." He spat the last part. His breathing was heavy. "So sure, take this train to the meeting spot. They deserve everything I give them, and a whole lot more."

"That they do."

"This war's got to end, you know. One way or another, it's got to end."

"I've been in war, son," I said, holding up my metal arm. "Lost some of myself to war. I know how it's fought. There's something folks don't tell you, though." I met the gaze of each of Jones's men in turn, ending with Jones himself. "There's only one way to win a war, and that's to be just one step worse than the other side. Use one bomb bigger. Or one gun faster. Use the disease they don't dare."

Jones took a step forward, his gun hand relaxing noticeably.

If I were going to shoot him, now would be the time. "We'll do what it takes."

"Sure," I said. "So long as you understand that means losing part of what it is you want to protect." I held his gaze for several tiny fractions of eternity. "Francis," I said. "Show these men out."

The last car split from ours and braked as hard as that little car could brake. Metal screeched against metal as its antigrav cut, and it dropped to the metal rails. The men inside tumbled, slamming against the forward walls—except for Jones.

Jones, as close to the door as he was, fell out of the front, his hand just touching his weapon as he tumbled in a mess along the tracks. Bones broke and blood flew. The man was torn and battered. His gun flew free.

Wind cracked around me, suddenly swirling around in a torrent now that it came in the new last car of the train. I braced myself against the wall, suddenly unsteady.

Then the world went black. The tunnel swallowed us as sure as hades itself swallowed the dead. Pressure pushed on my ears, and the air suddenly went musty and still. The train stopped.

"Rosa," I said. "Care to detonate the charge I placed on that last car?"

With a wicked grin, Rosa flashed up a small handheld computer. On it, she selected something from a list, confirmed her choice, and detonated the bomb. The flash of light shone down the long tunnel from outside.

I sat down right there on the back of the train. My legs wouldn't hold me anymore. The comedown after such an adrenaline rush made me feel older than I ever had. The bones in my hand ached like they'd been crushed in a vise. The bones in my whole body ached.

"That went well," Rosa said, sitting next to me.

"It ain't over yet," I said. I didn't know exactly what else was coming, but this sure as hell wasn't done. "Chester Goodwin's on his way, and we're right where he wants to meet us."

17

———

The air was cool and silent in the tunnel, like the barrel of a gun long since out of ammo. Far behind the train, a pinpoint of light burned in the black—the one indication that there might be some way out of this stone tomb. My lungs pulled in the musty stink—like wet tar mixed with old mold. The others moved around, bringing out lights so we could see if anyone came or went. Legs repaired a turret using the remains of other turrets. Rosa lined up the blockades, so we'd have cover if someone else attacked.

But nobody came.

"We just park here?" I asked.

Francis's voice came through a wave of digitized static. "Yes."

Something Jones had said bothered me right down to the marrow of my bones, but I couldn't get my head around it.

We'd killed Casket's gang. The images of that poor fool tumbling in a ruined mess in front of their train car played itself over and over every time I closed my eyes. What had he wanted that he'd been willing to die for it? A train heist on an unsuspecting target was one thing. Their assault had been a vicious attack on an aware and well-defended train.

They hadn't wanted to derail the train. If that had been the goal, they'd have bombed the tracks up ahead. No, they wanted to take the train back, fully functioning and full of its cargo.

The prisoners. What made them so special?

Trish swore behind me. Another failure at picking the prisoners' locks. These physical locks weren't any different in design than locks had been for hundreds of years. Each one was a keyed padlock holding together the black metal bars. The lockwork was slim and intricate, but any fool with a bent piece of metal could pick it if they'd had some. Trish, apparently, hadn't had much practice.

Spitting at every ache in my old body, I forced myself up to help. I grunted and held out my one hand capable of fine work, and she relented the tools. Picking locks had never been my favorite skill, and losing one hand made the whole challenge much more difficult. Still, there was a deep satisfaction inherent in picking a lock. Man versus metal, and with patience and finesse, man could prevail.

Thirty minutes later, I was muttering curse words I hadn't used in years. Keeping the pressure just right and feeling for the tumblers was wrecking my aching hand.

"I can feel it," I said. "It's almost there." I chewed my bottom lip and closed my eyes as I visualized the internal workings of the lock. "Here," I said to Trish. "Keep pressure on that. Gentle, though."

She complied. "Someone really didn't want these open."

Jones probably had the key. If I disconnected my skidder from the back of the train, I could be there and back in minutes. "You done well out there," I said.

"I had a clear shot and full ammo."

"That's not what I mean."

With her help, I dropped another tumbler into place. My heart pounded and my palms grew slick with sweat, but I couldn't take time to settle myself. Any slip and I'd lose the progress I'd made.

Then I made the mistake of opening my eyes. A child stared back at me, dull eyes staring right into my goddamn soul. He was young, probably less than ten. His hair hung around his cheeks like oily rags, and his feet were bare. It was all I could do to keep from flinching away and ruining the lock pick.

"You awake, kid?" I asked.

The child stared at me, unmoving.

"Who are these people?" I asked Trish.

When I hazarded a glance, I saw that Quin had returned as well.

"I don't know who they are. They're not registered anywhere." Trish shifted her weight, careful to avoid changing her pressure on the torsion wrench. "Why aren't you more concerned with where they're going?"

Quin said, "I don't like it."

"Well," Trish said, "it's not really up to us to like it or not. These people need to be freed."

"Even if they have the virus?" Quin asked.

"We don't even know there *is* a virus," Trish said. "All we got is Reginald's word and he's a damn liar."

The implication of her statement brewed in the back of my skull. If they were infected, then maybe they couldn't be saved. In fact, saving them might allow the disease out into the wild. But what if they weren't infected?

Another tumbler fell into place. "Reginald didn't tell us much about the disease, did he? I figure it's deadly, but what if it's not? And how's it transmitted?" My pick slipped, but it didn't wreck my progress. The tumblers stayed in place. "Maybe their blood is the payload, but if we get them a proper doctor they might survive."

"Look at them," Quin said, shaking her head. "There's something wrong in there. They don't speak and they look at us like they don't really understand what we're here for."

I said, "Not even sure if they can be considered trafficked if they won't give a statement."

"They can," Trish said. "Casket's gang was either trafficking humans or transporting human biomass. Either way, I'm glad we killed Casket and I'm not looking forward to my next conversation with Austin."

"Austin?" I regretted the tone in my voice the second it grumbled out.

"You're damn right. J.D., do you think I enjoy having to work with Goodwin? He's always had an interest in the outland, but he's the only one willing to keep Dead Oak alive."

I gritted my teeth. "The people of Dead Oak keep themselves—"

The last tumbler clicked into place, and the door slid open. There it was, the feeling I'd been missing. A deep, fulfilling sense of accomplishment. Man over metal—with a little help from a powerful woman. I found myself face to face with the kid in the train, his hollow eyes staring back at me and right through my soul. I'd set them free. We'd get them to safety.

So, why did I feel like dirt? Why did it feel like I was doing nothing for these poor, helpless people? The boy swallowed with a dry sound in his throat. What if touching them transmitted the disease. What if there was something wrong with them that made the whole lot of them dangerous? I met the kid's gaze, and I saw a spark of comprehension there—and fear.

I did all I could think to do. My arms spread wide, I waited for the young boy to step forward. He did—one shuffling step, then another. He reached out with pale fingers and touched first my big metal hand, then my human arm. He focused on my chin, no longer daring to meet my eyes. Then he stepped forward again and wrapped his arms around my chest in a hug.

I hugged him back, careful not to squeeze his skinny frame too hard.

"It'll be all right, kid," I said. "We'll figure this out."

We moved the freed prisoners off the train. They shuffled along like zombies, aware of their surroundings but not fully comprehending. When they were off, I showed Quin how to work the lock picks, and she took to it like she'd taken to every other challenge—with enthusiasm and not any small amount of natural talent. She had the next lock open in five minutes.

Three cars closer to the back, I found Legs and Rosa putting stitches in Sunset's back. Rosa worked with a cigarette dangling from her lower lip, needle tugging against Sunset's blood-slick flesh.

Sunset hardly winced, though it must have hurt like hell. "J.D., you better be here to tell me my bounty's dead and wrapped up in a nice package."

"Dead enough," I said. "Fella fell out of a train at more than a hundred fifty kilometers per hour."

Sunset's whole body shook, and it was Rosa who figured out what was happening before I did. "Quit laughing," Rosa said. "I'm trying to stitch you."

"No, it's fine, it's fine," Sunset said, grin on her face. "Just get that sheriff down here to transfer my stars and we'll be good."

"There's no signal to the outside here," Legs said. "No stars changing hands down here unless you got them in hard currency."

"We'll make it right," I said, continuing up the train. "Don't you worry."

The train was just as I'd left it. Blood smeared on the walls, bullet holes in the ceiling. The long walk through narrow aisles felt like a march into the underworld, each step harder than the last. My skin itched with anticipation, and my ears picked out every scratch-scrabble of noise in the rapidly cooling locomotive.

Because down in my gut, way deep down, I knew that something was wrong. I'd walked this road before, and more than once it'd ended going bad to worse. The air reeked of electricity and death: the raw, slick scent of the devouring machine.

"Trish," I said in the comm. "Walk the prisoners down track when they're free. We need to get them out of this tunnel."

For once, she agreed with a simple, "Will do."

Francis wasn't in the engineer's cabin. I looked around, poking at the ruins of the little room. The desk had been overturned, revealing a safe, which now stood open. The sofa had been torn to shreds and the art scoured from the walls. There was blood in the carpet, but in the dark I couldn't tell if it was Francis's fresh blood or a gift left over from my tussle with Jones.

I'd just walked the whole train, so I knew he wasn't anywhere on it. Where would he have gone? What was he up to?

I found my way out onto the petroleum-soaked gravel. Did I even bother to try to reach Francis on the comm? It seemed foolish, like that was just one more way to let him into my head.

"Francis," I said on the comm.

Silence.

I peered into the darkness in front of the train. The white headlight cut through the black, but it wasn't far before even that got swallowed in the oppressive dark.

"Francis," I said again. Still no response.

One foot found its way in front of the other, and soon I was out in front of that harsh headlight. Touching the gravel, I saw the fresh imprint of a narrow boot. He'd been this way—or someone had. There were other impression too, but it was impossible, in this place undisturbed by wind and rain, to determine how old any of the tracks were. The metal rail didn't even show wear, since the train floated above the tracks as it moved.

Quin came up alongside me. "Hey," she said, breathless.

"Don't you have work to do?"

"Locks are all open, and the others are handling the people. They sent me ahead to see what you're up to."

"They want you to babysit me?"

She grinned. "They said to keep you out of trouble."

"What about just using the comm?"

"Legs bet me that you'd never say that."

I stopped and turned to her. She had a smart look on her face. "Congratulations."

"Anyway, the comms aren't working."

They weren't. I realized it then. There wasn't the telltale hum of a connection when I toggled mine on. So, Francis hadn't been ignoring me. Or he had and he'd just extended his ignoring to include everyone. All at once, the thousands of tons of rock overhead started to feel genuinely smothering.

"So, what should we do?" Quin asked.

"You still got that gun?"

"Yeah."

"Bring it. We're going to go get ourselves into some trouble."

18

Exhaustion slugged me in the gut after we'd walked for five minutes in the black tunnel. Behind us, the train still stood, its harsh white light faded and far away. Quin's footsteps, silent in any other situation, now ground like landslides of gravel with each step. Every ache in my body told me to stop, but a burning need drove me forward.

"I don't think this is a good idea," Quin said. "We should go back."

Still, we walked.

Minutes passed. My boots scuffed against the metal rails—one step, then another. How long had it been since I'd had a decent sleep? Days? Years? It felt as if I'd never get a good rest ever again. My gut told me something was terribly wrong, but I couldn't figure out what. The certainty of it itched at my bones.

"Stop," I said. My voice thundered in the empty tunnel, then swallowed its own echoes.

Quin stopped.

"This ain't right." I knelt town and touched the gravel. It was slick with oil, as it had been the whole way through. "When they ran the tracks, they treated the gravel with the oil to keep it from getting too many weeds. Standard practice for this kind of tracks."

"Even underground?"

"Down in the tunnel it wasn't necessary, but nobody bothered to tell that to the workers." I lowered myself to the earth and peered across the level ground. "There's a lot of rules and regulations folks still follow, even if there's not a good reason."

Quin knelt down and touched the oil, rubbing it between her fingers. "So?"

"This stuff gets disturbed when someone steps on it." The way ahead was flat as the day it was first set. "This tunnel might as well be the surface of the moon."

She peered around, first on the side of the tracks where we walked, then on the other side. "There aren't any disturbances."

"We've missed them."

"Them?" She screwed up her face. "What them? What if they walked on the tracks?"

"They didn't." Retracing our steps, we headed back toward the train. I kept close to the wall, careful to run a hand along the contours of the rough-hewn stone until I found what I was looking for. A dark alcove, almost invisible from the other direction, but obvious as the sun in the sky from there.

"There's a door back there," Quin said, peering at the faint outline on the wall. She shot a glance back at the train, now a good distance away. She fidgeted in place, her fingers drumming on the barrel of her shotgun.

After some fiddling, I figured out where to push to open the door. There was a small shelter inside, something that the workers who built the tunnel probably used to rest. It had bunks on one side and the remains of a small cooking unit. At my signal, Quin lit her cube and shone the light around. The press of close tunnel walls disappeared as we stepped deeper into the room, and each scrape of boot against stone echoed high up into a vaulted ceiling too high to see. Far in front of us, at the very edge of Quin's light, I saw what I was looking for.

Francis stood watching from the shadows of some iron stairs.

Stairs. Metal construction, reaching up to a platform thirty feet above and beyond into the void.

"Jasper Davis Crow," said Francis.

"Why are you running, son?" I asked.

He spread his palms wide. "I do not run."

I didn't give that the dignity of a response. He knew better than anyone my inability to let things go. His whole wreck of a family was a testament to my hardheadedness. Plus, I didn't have enough breath left to give much of a shout back.

"We should leave," Quin whispered.

"No," I said. "I still think he's up to something." I took another step forward.

"You know," said Francis, voice echoing against the stone. "I thought about this a long time. Even without all the pain you tried to cause me, I still burned for justice."

"Justice," I spat, sure that Francis would never listen to my opinion on the subject. To Quin, I said, "All I ever did was try to find justice for that boy's dead father. Murdered by his mother." I took another step forward, then another. Quin's light flickered as she moved up behind me.

"What happens when this country is at war? You've fought in war, J.D. You've fought for peace, didn't you? We're not so different after all." Had I imagined the mirth creeping into Francis's flat tone?

"You wanted to make zombies out of the whole population using tech in their heads." I tapped my temple. "It was a monster's plan, and stopping you started this whole damn war."

Francis's voice sounded closer when he spoke next. "People like you thrive in war. You live for the fight, and without it you're nothing. You can't even conceive of a world of peace, where the lawmen aren't even needed. You don't know how to live if your honor isn't constantly driving you to fight."

Quin moved to one side, taking her light with her. The glow shone in Francis's eyes, his coyote eyes flicked to the girl passing behind me.

Francis stood immobile in the eerie light. My heart thundered in my chest, choking me with its cacophony. Instinct hit me again. Francis had something planned. He shifted his stance, and the glint of a weapon caught the light. He wore a pistol.

"Now," I said to Quin.

Her light went dark. I drew my small pistol, but my hand cramped.

Gunshots. The flashing strobes of hot brilliance blinded me as I rolled to the side. Noise like a thunderclap shattered the air. I raised my pistol to fire—but at what?

"Quin!" God, what had I done? My leg seized and I went down. I pushed forward. He moved past me in the dark and I lunged, missing him by centimeters.

Lights flared from above.

Someone moved behind me. I spun—raised my pistol.

And saw Quin standing there pointing her shotgun at me. Behind her, Francis stood, barely a shadow against the darkness.

"You'd best set that down," Francis said.

I holstered the little pistol. It wouldn't do me much good anyway.

Francis said, "Part of me thought you'd never make it this far."

Words stuck in my throat like lumps of molasses. I couldn't believe Quin would betray me like this. Worse, I couldn't believe that I didn't see it coming. She'd been there the whole way, making sure Francis was properly transferred. Keeping an eye on me whenever I wasn't being looked over by the psychopath himself. Now here she was, looking down the end of her shotgun at me.

"It was a gamble letting myself get captured," Francis said. "There was no guarantee you wouldn't just shoot me." He cocked his head almost imperceptibly. "Except, there is a guarantee, isn't there? You would never kill a man in cold blood. It's not something you are capable of."

"I am," I gasped. "I was."

"Well, it was a variable, wasn't it? Could this monster who's been tracking me for years actually go through with killing me?"

Quin wouldn't meet my gaze.

"Is that why you sent her?" I asked. "To kill me if I looked like I'd finish you off."

Francis was silent for a long time. His eyes flicked from me to Quin, and when he finally spoke, it was with barely a whisper. "She was there to remind you of yourself. Your conscience. I wasn't sure you had much left."

"I wasn't so sure either."

He shook his head. "War is killing Texas. This place is torn apart as long as nobody's willing to give up on this poisonous honor culture. Honor's nothing more than a reason to kill each other, but there just aren't enough of us left to matter. The war's got to end."

"You lured us here. All of us. Was the virus a lie?"

"It was," said another voice from somewhere in the darkness. It was a nasal voice, high and weak at the same time. A man in a brown suit stepped forward, lighting a cigar with a flick of his wrist. He had a bald pate and an underbite, but his eyes were cruel as ice. I recognized him. It was Chester Goodwin, older than last I'd seen him and a good deal paler. "The only way to end a war like this is to win it. Decisively."

Above, more lights came on along the roof of the giant storeroom. At its center stood an enormous rocket, sides painted with red, white, and blue stripes. High above the nosecone of the rocket, the gray ceiling bore an enormous painting of the American flag.

"What the hell is this?" I asked.

Quin stared up at the rocket. It may have been in my best interest to take the chance to disarm her, but I couldn't bring myself to do it. That rocket was too damn big.

"This," Goodwin said, "is old tech. It's a nuclear missile."

"Why? There's no way this still works." Chester Goodwin, owner of one of the most powerful corporations in the big city, had no use for a weapon like this. Did he?

The smile that spread across his face lacked anything like mirth. "Our problem subjugating the rest of Texas isn't the hardscrabble resistance. It never had anything to do with you and your people. The problem is that none of the corporations will focus an effort on you for very long." He gestured at the huge rocket. "This will provide focus."

"This will *kill* everyone."

Chester shrugged. "Nonsense. A glancing blow will do us little good."

Everything clicked into place. "You needed Francis to hack the security systems."

"It was trivial," Francis said. "They could have done it."

"Yes, but not fast enough. Already the train has been still for too long." Goodwin paced. Now that the whole room was lit, I could see several of Goodwin's bodyguards in hulking exosuits here at the back of the room. "And we don't need the missiles to work. The fuel should be perfect now that we have the tech from the Candle."

"Shit," I said. The deal Trish had tracked to Candlestick Crossing. It wasn't about weapons arming the gangs. It was about constructing a bomb—a bomb that would now have fuel. "This train is the only way to get anything into Austin."

"Once the bomb sits at the base of the Austin towers, the other corporations will finally find it in them to cooperate."

I took a step forward. I'd recovered some after the excitement, and now my thoughts tended toward something like survival. "You're handing over control of this to Francis William Brown?"

"We gave him what he wanted in a fair trade. He's a reasonable man."

"What did he want? Me? A shot at Casket Jones? Trish? Was Sunset part of this?"

"A bonus," Francis said. "Casket Jones wasn't part of it, but Sheriff Trish kept me from visiting the ranch for years. Kept me from my family. She deserves what she gets. Sunset became almost as insufferable as you after I killed her little brother in Swallow Hill, and I figured if I put you two together you'd be worse for it."

"You were right."

"I usually am."

My fingers brushed the handle of the small pistol I'd picked up in the train. If I was quick, I might get a few shots off before they gunned me down. Unfortunately, with my hand broken like it was, I couldn't call myself anywhere near quick.

"I wouldn't think too much about that," Francis said, looking down at my hand. "Your hand will shatter if you fire a gun."

Another slow realization crept over me. "You made it heal wrong."

"That's right. Your nanomachine controller can be hacked just like any other system. I'd expected you to figure that out sooner." A muscle twitched at the corner of his eye. He wasn't telling the truth—or he was only telling part of it.

"Quin," I said, desperate. "You don't gotta do this."

The look she gave me was almost pleading. "I do," she whispered. "I don't break promises."

"No. Of course not. I won't ask you to." I took a step back toward the door, raising my hands.

"Stop," she said, her voice firmer.

"Oh, just shoot him," Goodwin said, turning to leave. "He's been a pain in our asses long enough."

Quin glanced at Francis, who nodded.

Shit.

I took another step back, trying to make Quin look at me. There was nothing for me to say. No special words I could use to win back her respect. Nothing.

For all my time wandering in the deserts and plains all over Texas, I'd always tried to live a life of honor. I figured if there'd be anything in all those dangerous lands that would get me killed, it'd be my own bullheadedness for an honor system. When someone ran, I followed, even when most hunters would shoot their quarry in the back. When a gunslinger challenged me to a duel, I'd always accept.

I'd always win, but I'd always accept. Only a damn fool figured he could grow old living like that. I'd always been the damn fool who did it, but even I was surprised at how long it'd worked out. This was it. My time was running to an end.

My hand touched the doorway, and I felt escape within my grasp. Quin finally met my gaze, and in her beautiful brown eyes I read a world of apology and a cold determination all at once. She wasn't going to back down, because she wasn't the backing-down type.

Well, neither was I.

She leveled the gun at my chest, and she fired.

19

———————

First thing I noticed when I woke up was that I was breathing. I wasn't some rotting corpse in a dark room under a whole hell of a lot of rock. Second thing I noticed was that every breath I drew hurt so bad I wished I was a rotting corpse in a dark room under a whole hell of a lot of rock.

I peeled open my eyes, then, regretting the view it gave me of Legs's ugly mug, I closed them.

"He's alive!" Legs shouted, not bothering to back his face away from me first. "Can you believe it?"

"He's always alive," Trish said flatly. "Haven't seen anyone kill him yet."

In response, I let out a pained moan.

When I opened my eyes again, Trish was close to my face. "J.D.," she said, "do you think you can move?"

I didn't think I'd ever move again.

Trish leaned in real close and whispered, "It's just that Casket Jones is still alive, and it would be really nice to not be in this damn place when he starts finds out we have his prisoners."

That got my attention. I forced myself up into a sitting position. With my human hand, I dabbed at my aching torso. Fingers came back drenched in blood.

Trish plucked something off the outside of my coat. "Oh, you'll be fine," she said.

I peered at the little ball of metal held between her thumb and forefinger. "Birdshot?" I asked. My head spun. How in hell did Quin shoot me with birdshot?

The wounds on my chest were all shallow. They hurt like hell, but nothing had penetrated more than half a centimeter. Only the shot that hit where my coat was open actually found flesh, so really I didn't have much to complain about. I still complained. Anything that hit the coat was brushed aside like so much sand.

Trish helped me stand.

That's when I first saw the people. Filthy, disheveled prisoners shuffled past in a line, headed past down the long train tunnel. They were the men and women from the train. The kid I'd seen on the train nodded at me as he passed by.

"A few of them started talking," Trish said. "I don't know why most of them are acting the way they are, but they obey orders."

I touched the few lumps still lodged in my chest. I looked at the wall where I'd fallen through the door. It was closed and invisible again in the intermittent shadows. "Goodwin was here. He and Francis are making a bomb."

"You believe that?"

"I believe that I hurt, and to be honest I'm not sure about anything else." I reconsidered. "I also believe that Francis is behind all this. He's playing Goodwin like he played us."

"There's always more to it," Rose said as she followed up the back of the line. She had Sunset with her, the large bounty hunter limping along with support. "This is the last of them, Sheriff."

Trish tipped her hat to the woman. "We need to follow."

I raised an eyebrow. "You're not arresting her?"

"I'm prioritizing."

"Sure." My gut told me it was more than that. Trish always carried a certain tension in her posture, but there was something else now. "How did you know where I was?"

She placed a hand on my shoulder. "It's important to keep track of our elders. Out of respect."

I shrugged away from her. "You traced me?"

Her smile creased the corners of her eyes. "When we figured out Francis had slipped away, we decided to give you a ping."

My gut ran cold as ice. "How long?"

She must have seen the rage boiling behind my eyes, because her shoulders tensed. "What do you mean?"

"How long have you traced me?"

The look of fear in her eyes didn't make me proud. "For years."

My cussing might have woke the dead. "You know me, Trish. There ain't a single thing in all of Texas that I hate more than being traced. Not Francis, not bad whiskey, not the hot sun when there's nothing to drink." I slugged the wall with my metal fist, taking a large chunk of black rock out of it. "Years! Did Francis hack your trace? Is that why he was always two steps away? Was that how Sunset found me?" My chest constricted and breaths came in ragged gasps.

"It's your arm," she said in a deliberately calm voice. "It's always been possible to locate you through it. When I figured that out, all I needed was your serial number."

The bottom dropped out of my rage. I'd long since come to terms with the abuse that was my metal arm. To discover one more betrayal of my metal body was nothing more than another slab of rotten beef on the grill of my life.

Trish took hold of my human hand. "You're hurt. You need to go with Rosa and Legs and find a signal so you can get picked up and taken away."

"Jones is alive?" I said as we followed the tracks to the far-away light.

"He's not too happy either. We spotted him coming down the tracks. Figured it'd be better to abandon the train now that the prisoners are free."

"He alone?"

She shook her head. "He has a few men left, and—someone else is with him. Armored."

"Shit." That's all we needed. Armored goons, like the thugs out of Austin. Goodwin's men. They had the train, then.

We continued, her moving without any hint of exhaustion, and me limping. Weak. Maybe she hadn't been joking at all about calling me a ride. Looking down at myself, I saw that I was drenched in my own blood. The birdshot had done a hell of a number on my chest.

"We have to go after them," I said. "You and me, like old times."

When we neared the entrance, she turned light on the walls. Alcoves here branched into several side passages. Up ahead, Rosa was ushering people into the coves and settling them in for a long wait. We would need to return with a ride. These people couldn't walk home. Not in the shape they were in.

"What is this place, J.D.?"

"It's an old chimney rock back there," I said. "Out in the fields by the Brown Ranch. There have always been legends about this place. None of them said anything about an old nuclear missile silo, but that's what's there."

She stared back down into the empty void. Her only word was "Damn," but she used it several times.

"Goodwin put a bomb on that train, and he thinks Francis is the only guy capable of making that happen."

"Damn," she said again. "It'll never work. This tech has to be ancient."

"Tech's not a problem. Court fired up the old factory for some custom-ordered parts."

"The checkpoint in Dead Oak would have picked this up," Trish said, but she didn't look convinced. "Is this—"

"Yeah, it's probably what you were after in Candlestick," I admitted. "Would have been a lot better if you'd have stopped it there, and I'm sorry I got in your way. I was a damn fool.

She gave me exactly the kind of look I deserved. "Quin and I didn't just sit around waiting for you, you know."

My jaw tensed.

"We figured on taking a look around."

"Did you get caught?"

"Almost. That kid's got chops, you know. She's smart as hell."

"Quarterback," I said. The ache in my chest reminded me of the birdshot she'd hit me with. "She's quick and she's always got the next play figured out."

"Well, we didn't find anything."

"The checkpoint wouldn't have caught it," I said. "A nuclear bomb with no fuel?"

"Would have looked like a pile of useless junk," Trish finished. "Nobody would have recognized that old tech."

Rosa rounded a corner. "We can't stay here."

"Why not?" Legs slapped the solid rock wall next to her. "It's a solid bunker. We can barricade the door against Casket."

Rosa pressed her lips together in a tight line for several long seconds. Finally, she said, "All he has to do is be patient, and we'll be screwed."

He scrunched up his face. "Can he do that?"

I said, "Trish and I will scout ahead. Goodwin and Francis will hopefully be busy back there for a while." It still didn't square with me that Francis and Goodwin were working together.

We made our way carefully forward, taking each step with absolute caution. Even in my boots, I managed to keep the noise low, but it was nothing compared to the silence of the sheriff. She had both guns drawn and slipped through the shadows like a ghost.

There were lights in the long hall. Ancient bulbs flickered with a dim yellow glow, burning dust as they heated up. Where the tunnel branched, Trish quickly checked for traces of an enemy. Each time it came up clear. We moved past the people from the train. Legs and Rosa helped corral folks to one side.

The tunnel finally opened into piercing bright morning sunlight, which drove straight through a clear summer sky and deep down into my aching skull. A few hundred meters ahead on the track sat a black lump of a train with the Goodwin logo shining bright gold.

Trish grimaced as we stepped closer to the open sky. "Signal's back," she said.

"Can you call for backup?"

She scoffed. "There's never really any backup, Sheriff."

"Then how about a ride?"

"You said we're close to the Brown Ranch. Shall we see if your friend Ben will help?"

"He'll come," I said, "but it might not be worth listening to him moan about it."

"If we can get those people to safety, then I'll listen to all the bitching and moaning in the world. I certainly put up with you well enough." She holstered her weapons.

A bullet pinged off the rock next to me. Scrambling back, I pushed Trish deeper into cover. My heart slammed against my ribcage, torn in half between exhaustion and adrenaline.

"Did you see where it came from?" Trish asked.

I hadn't, but I had a fair idea based on where it hit. "You still have a signal?"

She nodded.

"Tell Ben to bring steaks."

Trish shot me a funny look, but by the tilt of her head and

the flash behind her eyes, I could tell she was sending something out. I only hoped the message would get through to Ben quickly enough. Time passed, and the minutes felt like hours. There was no way to know if the sniper was still out there waiting. Watching.

I kicked the wall in frustration. "Dammit, I hate being pinned down."

"Just be patient."

The sheriff bandaged my wounds using a medical kit she kept in a pouch on her waist. She checked each shallow wound, picking the shot out if she could. Her touch was tender and caring, as if all the trouble I'd caused her over these long years hadn't meant one shot of bad whiskey to her. I was thankful for that, but it hurts getting undeserved love. It ached.

"Thank you," I said.

"You've lost some blood," she told me, resting a hand on my chest. "She could have killed you."

"Not for this," I said, indicating the bandages. "Well, this, but also... Everything."

She met my eyes for a short eternity. "You believed in me when I needed it, J.D. That means something."

"I've been far worse than any of that was worth."

Trish slapped the last bandage in place a little too hard. "That you have, but I made a promise to help people, and dammit, I'm sticking with it even if it includes you."

Something clicked in my muddled brain. Quin had said something about a promise. Why hadn't she turned that shotgun on Francis instead?

Because she'd made a promise to him. She had promised to keep him safe—just like I'd promised to keep *her* be safe.

"All right," I said after the sun sat a little higher in the sky. "I'm done with all this." I drew my small pistol and checked the ammo. Plenty, I hoped, since I didn't have any spare for that weapon. "Go back and get the others. We need to be ready to move them out."

"I *just* bandaged you," Trish said, but she left to do as I said.

For once, I would have welcomed more of an argument. Not because I treasured every interaction with the indomitable Contrisha Chin. No, she'd always irritated me, no matter how much I grew to respect her. An argument would have been nice because sometimes even I can admit that what I'm fixing to do is stupid as hell.

Pistol in hand, I stood at the edge of shadow. Deep breaths slowed my heart and eased my ragged nerves. I couldn't step out there with my hands shaking, no matter how much blood I'd lost.

I stepped into the sun, metal arm held forward for protection. Squinting up at the hill, I saw the puff of smoke when the first shot was fired. The bullet pinged off my arm, right where the metal meets my shoulder. Almost a fatal shot, but nothing to me. Nothing at all.

So I ran. Cover wasn't far, and I slid into place just as the next shot whizzed by.

This time, I saw who was shooting. One of Goodwin's armored goons stood a hundred meters away, not bothering to relocate for cover. That made sense, since I didn't really have a weapon that would punch through his armored plate.

Low and fast, I circled the hill. When I came out from a gap in the rocks, the goon fired again, this time pinging another shot off my arm. The ricochet opened a cut in my side I cursed back the sting and hoped the wound wasn't too bad.

A hundred meters was a long damn run, but the distance reminded me of Quin and her football. I scooped up a rock, judged the distance, and threw.

Missed.

The goon shouted something at me. I set my hat on my

metal hand and poked it up. When the bullet whizzed past, I scooped another rock, stood, and threw.

The stone pounded him right in the chest, staggering him backwards. I leapt forward, sprinting up the hill until my breaths came in ragged gulps, then I dove behind a short ledge where the scrubby brush above would block his view of me.

Trish unleashed a barrage of cover fire.

He went on the move. Thundering footsteps pounded the rocks as he made his way down and around, trying to expose me from my cover. Too slow. Too loud. I scooped up another rock, and, having holstered my pistol, set my hat back on my head.

Suddenly football made a lot more sense. This was kinda fun. When he jumped down to my level, only thirty meters to one side, I let the stone fly. It soared through the air.

He dodged.

"You're supposed to catch it!" I shouted as I ducked behind more cover.

Again, he tried to circle around, his route taking him to lower ground. I hugged the hard limestone ridge, keeping low so he'd still have trouble getting a clean shot at me.

He came closer. Had he lost sight of me?

Closer.

Too close. I reached over the ledge, extending as far as I dared, and grabbed his hand, gun and all. With an effortless squeeze, I crushed the whole mess, making a ruined lump of hand and gun alike.

He screamed, but I didn't let it bother me too terribly much. Jumping down behind him, I jammed a metal hand up under his back armor. The plates separated, screeching against my effort.

I drew my small pistol, squeezed it between the armor plates, and fired one shot.

The goon shuddered and went still.

The pistol felt warm in my hand—and good. It had hardly

kicked at all, and even with my hand in bad shape, this weapon was easy to manipulate. It wasn't powerful by any means, but I could fire it without pain.

I stood atop the rocky hill, looking out upon the windmill fields below. A dusty wind tugged at my coat, pulling it east like the insistence of a lost lover. My hat kept the sun off my face, and all of Texas lay out before me as a land ravaged by the uncaring monsters who had lived it for so long. Did anyone really want to save this place? Did I?

Goodwin said he wanted to unite his city, but he'd do it with violence. Francis—nobody knew what Francis wanted. He would scour the land clean without a second thought about who it hurt, because he *couldn't* hurt. Maybe a man's soul was only as good as the pain he could feel.

To my left, I spotted running horses, maybe some of Ben Brown's own herd. They'd have free reign of his lands, and this was the edge of it. I started walking down that way, sure that the horses would flee as soon as I approached.

Had I spared Francis's life because it wasn't honorable to kill an unarmed man? Or had I let him live because the pain he brought felt like penance for my own sins?

The hot sun warmed my soul and scoured my bones clean of exhaustion and ache. This was my Texas, and maybe her people didn't care to tend her like they should, but that didn't mean I couldn't try. I'd stop that bomb. Hell, I'd stop the whole damn war if I could.

"Dammit," I said. "Casket Jones was right."

A wave of heat hit me from above—not the searing glow of the morning sun, but a pulse of blue-hot flame. I looked up, squinting against the furious light.

"You're damn straight I was right," said Casket Jones from atop my skidder. "You're damn fucking straight!"

He grabbed me by the coat and with a twist of his wrist launched us both high into the air.

20

Blue flame scorched my boots and leg. We were a thousand meters up in seconds.

"We could have ended this war!" Jones shouted. "You're a goddamn traitor!"

Then he let go.

I grabbed the skidder's hot thruster with my metal hand and dangled there for a long second. Jones drew his red pistol and leveled it at me.

Swinging hard, I crossed to the other side of the bike underneath and launched myself up. My back pinged with pain and my muscles protested, but my boot connected with a crunching a kick at his knee.

The bike spun in the sky and dropped hard. In a moment of weightlessness, I climbed to face my enemy. Casket Jones's twisted face sneered as I heaved my body up. One side of his head was a mess of pink flesh, regrown recently. His shoulder and arm were charred like summer brisket, the threads of his fancy shirt scorched away from his left forearm. Sharp teeth showed in a wicked sneer, a result of his lips and cheek on one side having been burned black. He had survived the train explosion, but the ugly bastard would never be the same.

His eyes boiled with seething hate. "We had it won!" he shouted over the wind.

Below, the fast-spinning black windmills grew closer. "You're a slaver, Jones. Texas never wins when we're locking up innocents."

"They were prisoners of war!" He cranked the controls at the last second and slowed our fall. "Goodwin's men!"

He twisted his pistol around to point at me, but I held him back with my human hand. Without letting go, I could do nothing else. "You had kids in there."

An emotion flashed across his face that was hard to interpret. Guilt? Fear? "We couldn't separate them from their parents. We're not monsters."

Now, my own rage surged up. "Then you don't fucking arrest them. They're people looking for work." I shoved him hard, anger giving me the strength to fight. He twisted to deal with me, and his back smashed against the motorcycle controls.

The bike burst forward as both rockets flared. My foot slipped, and the world blurred. We dipped down into the rows of windmills, black giants whizzing past us at breakneck speeds. I released Jones's arm and grabbed the handlebar.

If I let go with my metal grip, all that held me there was that weak, broken hand. One punch, one slip, one mistake and there wouldn't be enough meat left on me to feed the first coyote who wandered past. Without my metal hand's solid grip on the rocket, I'd be dead in seconds.

But it had to be done.

I let go of the bike with my metal arm and took a wide swing at Casket Jones's skull. He had to be stopped.

Too damn slow.

He ducked, rolling with the strike. The bounty hunter swung his pistol around and pulled the trigger. Red-hot muzzle flare flashed across the patch over my bad eye, but the bullet missed. The skidder twisted around and we slowed.

My hand slipped. Pain rose like a river of molten iron up my arm, nerves twitching and weak from the fury of my abuse—but I held tight.

I swung again with the metal arm, this time grabbing his upper arm and crushing it with all the strength of the Texas Army's enhanced augmentation. He screamed in pain and fury. The red pistol fell and banged against the swinging arm of a windmill as we passed.

I shifted, holding onto the speeding bike with the heels of my boots so that I could reach the controls. Jones took the opportunity and punched me in the gut with his good hand. Bandaged wounds tore open under each strike.

"Francis said this would work," Jones said through his twisted lips. "He said this could end the war."

I pressed my face close to his. "There's nothing more to that man than lies."

Jones shook his head. "Francis Brown is a hell of a lot more honorable than you or me."

Letting go of his crushed arm, I swung my big metal arm so I could get another punch at him. Instead, as I pulled it back, a windmill arm slammed against it, nearly pulling me free of the bike. Shit, how'd that get so close? Thirty meters of air swung around under me as the whole bike shifted under the force. The earth loomed over my head as we careened to the side. Casket landed another gut punch and my grip with my heels went weak.

I got a handful of his ruined shirt with my human hand and pulled. The bike righted, then spun. Something went wrong with the thrusters. We hovered. Over the droning hum of the windmills and the furious gales of wind, a thundering rumble sounded. Something far-off, something big approached through the dust-thick stench of the dry Texas desert.

"You're a damn coward!" I hollered over the noise of an approaching windmill blade, pressing back against the pressure he put on me. The ground swung around under me again, the windmill blade whipping past.

He tried another swing at me, but I held him too close to get proper leverage.

"What was Reggie making?" I screamed in his face to be heard now, the windmill arms passing only a meter from where we hovered.

He laughed through bloody teeth.

"What is it!?"

"It's a cure for Texas." His eyes held pure hatred. Pure rage. When he spoke again, it came with ragged resignation. He pointed at his face. "Reginald did this to me, J.D. His experiments for Goodwin led to a cure for bullet poisoning." He laughed a high-pitched laugh. "It worked, too, but it was too much. Made me immune to implants of any kind, but I could heal from damn near anything." The windmill blades swung closer, wind pulling at my hat. "Except then the tumors came. The cancer, old man. Always the goddamn cancer."

I remembered the lab equipment Reginald had in the train. It wasn't a miracle cure he was working on. This had to be something else. "What about the bioweapon?"

He let up some, his grip on me relaxing a hair. "Oh, it was going to be so good. He had those folks in his lab—the ones that don't talk. They're *fixed* he said. Obedient."

"Quiet."

"He took their will, their voice, their tech." Jones's broken face twisted into a sneer. "All that at Goodwin's orders. Wouldn't it be great if we hit Goodwin and all of Austin with the same bioweapon he meant for us?"

"Something like that shouldn't exist at all."

"But it does," Jones said. "Reginald uses it to make obedient servants of regular folk. So I made him fix a version for me."

"Make it better?"

"Better?" He laughed bitterly again. "More than just better. He made it perfect. He made the virus powerful enough to heal me from anything shy of a head wound. No side effects—no cancer."

"We burned everything he made," I said, waiting for the words to sink in. "We torched the bombs and every dose except for the one we couldn't find. Did you take that dose?"

Jones laughed. He laughed and laughed, and when I thought he couldn't laugh anymore, he switched to a burst of fury, shoving me back and shifting once again the movement of the skidder. We swayed to one side, and the spinning blades passed dangerously close to my head. I swore and slammed a fist into his broken face, sending blood and pain through my wounded hand. It hurt like hell, and the agony woke me to the life poor Jones was living.

He had been experimented on. Casket Jones hadn't asked for the twisted healing he was getting. If anyone had a right to hate Goodwin—hell, hate all of Austin—it was Jones. They'd taken him as a soldier, experimented on him, and sent him on his way to swim in a pool of constant agony. Eternal pain of a body that rejects itself on an ongoing basis. His bones weren't just always healing. They were healing and then growing cancerous, forcing him to fix himself with surgery, which caused more so-called healing.

Which caused more cancer.

War was a cancer on Texas, tearing it apart. Far be it from Casket Jones to try just once to put an end to that war. An end to that cancer.

But what he said wasn't going to work. There was no head to cut off. Goodwin didn't rule all the corporations waging their own private wars against the various peoples of the outlands. Cut that head off and there were a dozen more to rise up. No, Casket Jones had a different plan.

Infection. Make the people of Austin reject the very technology they relied on. Twist them in a way that made them less likely to fight for the dwindling resources of the desert land. What would the people of Austin do if they all got infected by Reginald's worst version of the virus? The effect would be profound and unpredictable, but would it be a bad thing?

"Where's the final dose?" I growled over the thundering noise all around. It grew to a roar and swallowed my words, so I shouted again, "Did you take that last dose?"

He took a swing at me, and we dipped closer to the spinning windmill blades.

"Where's the last goddamn dose?"

"That was the good dose," he said. Tears welled in his eyes. "That was the last good dose."

"Where is it?"

"You!" Jones shouted. "You fucking ruined everything!"

He twisted free and wrenched backward to hit the controls. The bike lurched toward the top of the windmill blade's swing, headed straight for the swinging arm. As it came, I saw death closer than I ever had, the whirling, obliterating ferocity of the power-generating device. In that split second, my brain had to weigh the choice of an easy death or a difficult life.

Because life was always difficult. Pain and suffering always ended when life slipped from a person. It was the one mercy I could give a poor suffering fool like Casket Jones. Hell, he'd taken that mercy himself, without my assistance.

It wasn't like anyone would blame me for dying. Who would miss me? I'd always been a pain in Trish's side. She'd mourn my loss the way a person mourns the loss of a particularly unruly horse. No, she'd be fine. Quin had betrayed me, she wouldn't suffer much. Hell, Legs and Rosa probably wouldn't miss me all that much either.

All this consideration, in the final fraction of a second before the whirling blades, only resulted in me realizing that there was some small shred of this life that made me want to live. I'd promised myself I'd do whatever Texas needed to heal. It wasn't the noble cause that brought me the will to survive, but the promise.

One goddamn promise.

I jumped as hard as I could, launching myself up from the skidder as it sped into the whirling windmill. My force pushed it down as it plunged into the spinning death, and I leapt up and over as the blade crashed hard into the bike. That black blade brushed against my coat, and finally, the wind snagged the hat from my head.

The skidder exploded in a blue-hot thunderclap. It vaporized Jones and struck me hard, sending me over and past the windmill.

And I fell. Gravity remembered me, tugging me down as fast as it always did. Hitting me with a kind of brutal fairness that had always felt like justice when I believed like such things.

About halfway down, I realized that the thing far below me wasn't hard dry earth.

It was cattle.

I hit that steer hard, the whole force of my body thudding onto the back of that glorious beast. I bounced off, wind knocked out of my lungs. Ribs cracked. The ground rose up and hit me hard as it ever did to anyone who ever thought to fall from the back of a giant bison-cattle hybrid.

The herd wandered past me, hooves thundering on the hard earth. They could step on me. Easily. My body wouldn't move. Lungs refused to work. I remembered the trampled body of Daniel Brown, Francis and Ben's father. The beasts didn't bother looking where they stepped. Once one's that big it doesn't much matter.

Finally, the herd passed, and Ben Brown rode up on his horse, looking down at me with sorrow on his face. He dismounted and knelt down next to me, my hat in his hands.

"Damn, J.D.," he said. "Never thought you'd actually die."

He knelt there, eyes closed in apparent prayer. The man thought I was dead, and despite my suspicions, he seemed to actually mourn my death.

"A betting man would have put me dead ages ago," I said.

He opened his eyes and stared at me, slow realization breaking over his face in waves. Relief. Anger. Disbelief. Finally, joy. Ben helped me to my feet, and I placed my hat back on my head.

Ben peered up at the windmill, spinning high above. "I can't believe you survived that," he said.

"Don't get ahead of yourself," I told him, stretching to test my range of movement. It wasn't good, and most any movement sent tweaks of white-hot agony through my ribs. "I'm fixin' to go get myself killed."

21

———

Ben brought the skittish gelding for me to ride, and the horse had allowed me to mount. It wasn't a fast horse, and riding him made me miss Muffin more than anything. Still, riding was better than walking.

Not by much, though. Every step that horse made sent searing waves of pain through my ribs. Aching fire burned fierce all along the left side of my body. The joint where my metal arm contacted the flesh of my body sent ripples of tingling pain up my spine every time with every single step.

Jones's words echoed through my head. He was dead for real this time, verified by the burned chunks of skull scattered around the windmills. My beloved skidder—shit, Trish's beloved skidder—was destroyed in that blue explosion. That loss hit me harder than I'd expected. The bike had meant freedom for me for a long time. I'd once loved it almost as much as I loved my horse.

My own horse. Not this damn gelding. He stepped up to a cantor again, the change in rhythm sending fresh knives of fire through my bones. After I swore enough, he slowed to a walk.

Ahead of us, Ben's herd of gigantic cattle thundered slowly

along until we reached the edge of the windmill power farm. They turned on their own, bending along the edge of the Brown property as if trained.

"You got my message," I said once Ben was close enough to hear.

"Bring steaks." Ben adjusted his hat. He wore a Stetson like mine, but his was black as a moonless night. "Figured I was leading them out anyway, might as well swing by."

"Still got them under control?" I asked.

"They're not chipped or anything, if that's what you're asking. I give them conditioning, but there's no metal in their heads."

"Good." He knew as well as I did that Francis could turn any technological controls of the giant beasts against us in no time at all. Last thing we needed was an enemy-controlled stampede of the thousand-kilo, half-bison longhorns.

"Why'd you want them, anyway?"

"Figured we could move them in position to slow down that train."

He scowled at me, the hard muscles of his jaw twitching with irritation. It was a damn fine scowl.

"I know, I know—you don't want your cattle hurt. I'm talking about blocking up the tunnel so as they can't get the train moving. Once that thing gets going, there's not much we can do, but if we keep it from starting, nobody gets hurt."

"So, what's in this train?" Ben gave a whistle and the herd bent a little around to the right, headed straight for the tunnel exit. "What's so special you can't let it go."

"You ever heard of a culture of honor?" I asked.

He shot me a look. Of course, he had.

"Someone comes and steals a horse from you, what's the best thing you can do? Forgive him? Or do you hunt him down, take back your horse, and make him pay?"

"You're going to tell me to forgive."

"Hell no. You forgive that guy, and he'll be back for another horse. When someone insults you, best thing to do is fight them for it, no matter how outmatched you might be. You back down once, then they know you're a target. That, son, is called a culture of honor."

"That's just normal culture. It's just how the world works."

"Sure," I said. "Sure. But I've been thinking on this. Feuds start like this, with bloodied noses turning into broken limbs and then murders. Generations later, people are still pissing at each other fighting over something nobody remembers. I've seen it a hundred times out there, some stupid offense growing into full-on war. Hell, I don't know that there's ever been a war didn't start like that."

"Even your civil war?"

I glanced down at my metal arm. The Texas Civil War had been a hell of a fight, and I'd believed it with all the passion in my soul when I'd fought in it. "Thing is," I said, "this new war looks a whole lot like that one, only now I'm old enough to see how all the pieces fit together."

"Funny," he said. "I never thought the pieces fit."

"Maybe they don't."

We crested a rise and the tracks laid out before us, emerging from the rocky hill where Goodwin's train still sat like a black blotch in the noonday sun. From where we stood, I could see that they'd moved the other train forward, and it looked like they might be attaching the two. That meant they'd already loaded up the fuel from that American rocket.

I drew my gun as the gelding walked endlessly forward. First, I checked my revolver with the single Red Number Five, the bullet I'd saved for Francis. My chest ached at the idea of finally killing that kid, but it might come to that. It probably *had* to come to that. I wouldn't back down this time. He was dangerous, and he'd always be dangerous.

I'd bloodied that man's nose years ago, and he was a damn fool for not making me pay for it.

The little pistol I'd taken still had fifteen bullets—small ones, but decent enough quality as far as I could tell. The action was smooth and the barrel still smelled of burned oil. It'd been cleaned recently. Good.

The thought of firing another gun at another person made my joints hurt. There'd been too damn much violence in my life. For all I'd done to chase justice, I'd only ever really managed to make more pain. Somehow this endless feud I had with injustice never deescalated itself. It never would.

"J.D.," Ben said. "Are you listening to me?"

"What?" He'd been talking, but I'd tuned him out.

"Maybe I should have fought you that first day you came to the ranch," he said. "Fought you that once so you'd know not to keep coming back and taking things from me and my family."

I grunted my assent. Made sense.

"Anyway, if you aren't too bothered, the train's moving."

"What?" I maneuvered my horse up a slope so I could see around the massive wall of cattle ass in front of us. Ben was right. The trains, together, had started to move. "Shit."

"What happens if they get away?"

Urging the gelding forward, I said, "They don't get away."

"Maybe you don't understand the hypothetical—"

I grabbed a handful of his coat and looked him straight in the eye. "They don't get away. They can't." The closest longhorn let out a long, irritated bellow. "How do we get these moving?"

"We can't—"

"How do we get them moving?" My raw voice sounded more desperate than I intended. "Ben, this is big. End of the war. Maybe end of Texas." Far away, the train wasn't moving fast. It crept along, its movement barely perceptible but for the glimmer of its reflection of the hot summer sun, like a chrome snake slithering through fire.

That got me thinking of the snake Francis, and all the manipulating he'd been doing. What did he want? What exactly was his goal in this whole game? Goodwin wanted him to activate the nuke. Casket Jones had wanted him to spread a disease. Francis wanted—what?

Only one word came to mind when I put myself in Francis's shoes.

"Revenge," I said.

"What?"

"Ben, I figured it out. Francis controls the bomb on the train. He has Trish right there. Goodwin will be dead. Hell, he's always had something against you. Francis wants to stick a knife in everyone who's ever wronged him."

"And he's got you."

"He's always had me. Every goddamn step he takes twists the knife in my side."

He scratched his chin. "I don't know. That doesn't feel right."

I whistled loud as I could. The cattle put on a surge of speed. "Hyah!" I yelled, and whistled again.

More speed, but not enough.

"Sorry about this, Ben."

I pulled out the small pistol and shot the slowest steer in the ass. It let out a yell of rage and the whole mass surged forward. The gelding picked up the energy of the herd and followed.

"What the fuck!" Ben shouted, urging his horse to catch up. "What are you doing?"

I shot another beast, and the herd broke into a run. Earth shook under their hooves, rocks cracking. The sky was choked in dust and fear. The stampede had started. Cattle ran across the desert flats, where the hard packed earth was barren, cracked clay. The herd didn't slow, it didn't turn, it just moved in the relentless fury of a driven will.

My will.

But it still wasn't fast enough. Far away, the train slid along its tracks. Faster and faster it flashed in the sun. It would still be gone by the time the cattle crossed. Long gone before we could do a damn thing in its passing.

And once it was all the way out of the tunnel, Francis would detonate the nuke taking out Dead Oak and the Brown Ranch. He'd even irradiate Austin, maybe enough to make the last Texas city uninhabitable.

Shouting, I veered to the right, around the flank of the thundering stampede. Ben whistled, a sharp staccato trill, but the herd ignored him. I got up on the balls of my feet into the stirrups, trying my best to soften the painful blows from my galloping horse. It didn't help much, but adrenaline from the ride surged through my veins and pulsed in my skull. I shot a steer in the side, and it turned.

The whole herd turned with it, pulling hard to the left.

Too hard. Dammit. I dropped back. We were getting close, tracks drawing near like a silver slash across the red rock. Where was Ben?

Gunshots. Ben drove the herd from the other side. I let out a whoop and waved my hat in the air. We were on course. Faster. Faster.

A specimen of Texas cattle is a damn thing to behold, majestic and intimidating all on its own standing there. Walking, it was an imposing force that nobody stopped for nothing. Running? Hell, nothing that big ran without serious damage happening on the other end. The earth shattered and whole trees could be crushed like twigs. All of Texas trembled.

We had a hundred head running all out when we hit that train.

There's no technology in Texas that can hold up to a stubborn force like ours. A hundred longhorns bellowed rage like a hurricane of muscle and bone.

They hit the side of that train and it twisted with a sound like a thousand lightning strikes. Metal screamed against metal and the thunderclap after must have been heard a thousand kilometers away.

The train crumpled like it was made of foil, bending in on itself. Horns tore through thin metal flesh and rent machinery to ruble and ash. The cattle flung that train far from the tracks and sent cars tumbling like toys across the broken Texas soil. Cars near the back of the train whipped from their tracks, snaking back past the cattle.

And right at me.

I pulled my horse up short, and he reared up—barely missed by the rear car.

He nearly threw me, but I held hard. When he'd stopped skittering and the train stopped its crashing, I urged him forward toward the wreckage.

"It's time to finish this," I said to Ben. "This has been due for a good long while."

"What has?"

"Francis William Brown!" I shouted. "I'm calling you out!"

22

———————

The crow landed atop a burning mess of train. It flapped its wings, annoyed by the very insult of the ruined technology around it. When I saw it there, our eyes met, and I knew that we'd reached the end. I dismounted and strode forward as if nothing in the world would stop me.

"Francis William Brown!" I yelled.

Far away, something exploded.

The herd of cattle lowed, agitated. They scattered, most lumbering toward the ranch. A few were in no shape to move, ruined by the crashed train.

Screams tore through the crackle of fire in the wind. Bloody, gut-grinding, painful screams. It hurt to think of the pain someone was in.

It was goddamn Chester Goodwin. That sniveling city man with designs on the domination of all Texas. His voice bled raw with screaming. I spotted him pinned by a ruined car. With my metal hand, I lifted the train from his legs, and he squirmed free.

Goodwin never much mattered to me at all, I realized, looking at him writhing in the dirt. His legs weren't so bad as I thought they'd be, but he squirmed like a severed worm. Him and all of Austin could go on living their lives, wrecking them if they must. They'd been the enemy of a war fought long ago—a war nobody had won. Now people kept up the war—why?

"This war ends," I said to Goodwin once he was done hollering.

"Never," he said through gritted teeth. "Not till you're dead."

I blinked. "Me?"

"All of you. Dead or finally under control. Austin can't afford to let you soak up the resources left to us."

I drew my weapon and leveled it at his head. "Son," I said, "you'd best consider what this war is worth to you. If Austin and the rest of Texas works together, there's plenty to go around."

He held out a hand for me to shake. I took it, and he gripped tight. My blood smeared across the ruins of his fancy suit. "You're the one he picked, aren't you?" he said. The way he looked at me prickled.

I pulled away from his grip. "I'll talk with you later."

"It's all Francis Brown, isn't it?" he said as I walked away. "He's outsmarted us all." His laugh hit a manic pitch before being drowned out by another explosion in the distance.

At the mention of Francis's name, rage gripped me all the way through, and all I saw was the blood-red haze that stripped all other options down to nothing. Only violence remained.

Goodwin was right about one thing. My beef was with Francis. That man had orchestrated this whole thing. He'd drawn his enemies to that train and when he got us there, he'd led us straight into his trap. It wasn't the easiest way to kill us all, but what did that matter to an insane man like Francis William Brown? His goal was revenge—it had to be—and revenge took twists and turns that simple murder never bothered with.

Hate a man and slit his throat. Thirst for revenge and make him watch everything he loved burn before you grace him with a bullet in the skull.

The fact we weren't all dead only further convinced me of

the man's insanity. He was always a broken brilliance, but the closer I looked, the more I saw the fissures in his shattered mind.

"Francis!" I shouted again. "Get your ass out here!"

It had all started when he decided to let me capture him. He'd made sure everything fit—he made sure I wouldn't kill him. He knew about the bounty and where I'd take him. He'd already arranged things between Goodwin and Jones. All he needed was a force on the inside able to tweak things if they started to go sideways.

Quin stepped out from behind the flaming wreckage of a car, shotgun leveled at my chest. Atop the train, the crow cawed in irritation.

"Get out of here, kid," I said to her.

She set her jaw but didn't speak.

"She promised to be my bodyguard," Francis said as he, too, emerged. "Promises are important, aren't they?"

There wasn't a damn thing Francis could have said that would cut deeper. I'd once promised to keep him safe. I'd sworn I'd save his mother. My first gut instinct told me he'd made a liar out of me. It wasn't true. I'd done that plenty all on my own.

"Francis," I said, my voice a low rumble in tune with the roaring flames. "I'm calling you out."

He took a step back. His eyes blinked rapidly. This hadn't been what he expected. "Excuse me?"

"A duel," I said. "You and me."

He stood without comment for a long time. When I was fixing to repeat myself, he said, "You can't possibly win."

Another train car exploded, this one close enough that the heat wave from it washed over the both of us like the rays of the noonday sun.

Quin took a step in my direction. "J.D., he's fast."

"Sure," I said.

"Your hand is hurt."

"True."

She looked at me, then at Francis, then at me again. "Why didn't you leave?" She glanced down at her shotgun. "I mean, I thought that you would, after—"

"Not without Francis," I said without taking my eyes off the man. "I made a promise to that effect, and the promises we make to ourselves are the most important ones. When he was a boy I said I'd always be there for him, and right from the beginning he was my mess to clean up. Now, you might have your deal with him that needs to be worked out, but the rules of honor say that now that I've called him out, there's only one way forward for him."

"To take the duel," Francis said, the flatness of his voice cracking. "And kill you."

"We should have walked this road a long time ago, son," I said.

The crow stretched its wings again, irritated by the smoke pouring from the ruined train. I clenched my fist, acutely aware that the joints still ached like they were full of sand. The muscles were still stiff. I'd once been a fast draw, but even at my fastest I probably couldn't have beat Francis. That didn't matter much. Whatever was wrong with my hand wouldn't clear in the next few minutes.

Or, I thought, maybe it would. Maybe death cures all ills.

Francis pulled his ragged hair back and tied it behind his head. He wore a gun belt, something he had no doubt taken from one of the fallen men. The gun on it was a sleek black, something new and quick and powerful. It was everything a modern man might look for in a weapon.

"I accept," Francis said.

Quin shot me a pleading look, but the time for pleading was long past. I set my jaw and hardened my heart. What happened next was what I'd always known would happen.

If it wasn't destiny, then it was something worse. Dying in a gunfight wouldn't make me the man I'd always been destined to be, but anyone who lives like I do is all but guaranteed this particular end.

I shrugged off my coat and folded it. There was no use in having more holes poked in the fancy duster. I handed it to Quin. "Take this," I said. "It's yours if I'm not needing it anymore."

She nodded solemnly.

I squared off against Francis and looked him straight in his cold eyes. He was still the haggard, ruined man I'd known since he was a broken kid. His eyes betrayed no emotion and his mouth pressed in a long, tight line.

"Hold it!" Trish said as she emerged from the tunnel.

"Trish," I said, "this has to happen this way."

Legs and Rosa emerged as well. Trish waved them along to go help Goodwin.

Trish stepped up to me and looked me straight in the eyes. Her jaw was pressed tight, and her hard expression told me she was done messing around. "We're doing this right," she said. "No fucking around."

Trish paced off the dueling grounds, marking off each end so the backdrop wouldn't shoot anyone or ricochet bullets off the burning trains. When that was done, she pulled us in close.

"You boys both really want to do this?" she asked.

Francis nodded.

"Sure," I said.

"No." Her voice was like ice. "Don't give me 'sure,' J.D. I need a real affirmative."

"This is where it's been headed for years. Ain't no way out of it and there never has been."

Her eyes peered right down into my soul. "There's plenty of ways out. You could step down. I could arrest him."

"You couldn't," Francis said, as if stating a truth as obvious as the color of the sky.

"I got one condition," I said after a moment of thought.

Francis gave a little shake of his head. "You're in no position to negotiate."

"I have a sheriff here and plenty of friends on my side."

"I have Quin," Francis said without a hint of malice. It was hard to gauge if he meant Quin was his enforcer or his hostage.

"That you do," I said. "That you do." Out of the corner of my eye, I saw Quin's grip tighten on her shotgun. "But this doesn't have to be ugly. My only condition is that I want to duel you."

Francis spread his hands, palms out. "Here I am."

Trish stepped back and folded her arms, peering down her nose at us like she disapproved of our childish behavior.

"No," I said. "All of you. When you came out of that coffin I put you in, you were a whole man. The tech in that coffin kept your emotion limiters disabled. What did you experience in there?"

He blinked hard, squinting out the noonday sun. After a long while, he said, "Delusions and madness, old man. Same as anyone else broken up by a hormone bath and a stasis coma."

"Hormones don't explain it." I stepped forward and looked him in the eyes. "You were having real feelings, and if you had them then, you can have them now. That's who I want to fight. That's who I challenged."

His eyes flicked to me, almost meeting my gaze before dancing away. "I'm not like other men," he said. "I'm much angrier, and it's dangerous."

"Is that why you're going to nuke Dead Oak?"

"What?" Trish said.

This time Francis's eyes searched mine, as if looking for some secret clue hidden there. "There's no nuke."

"No nuke, no bioengineered weapon. What else isn't there?"

Francis glanced at my hand, so I raised it in front of me. Purple and black bruises covered the swollen hand, and the scratch where Francis had clawed me still stood out like a blazing red flame.

"Turn your emotions back on," I said to Francis. "Turn your pain back on. It's only fair we fight on even ground."

Trish pulled me away from the dueling ground and whispered in my ear. "J.D., what are you doing? You're not this cruel, are you? Do you just want him to suffer when he kills you?"

I shrugged. "It is what it is."

"What would that be?" She wasn't going to back down, I saw it in the set of her jaw.

It hurt having to admit the truth to her. Hell, it hurt admiring the truth to myself. "I'm demanding something unreasonable so he'll back down. You're right. This was stupid."

"You want to let him go?"

"Want? Not really. Honor pushes me forward, Trish, but I don't know what's right anymore. Something I realized when I fought Jones is digging at me now that I've calmed down some."

"You figured out you've been a jackass all these years?"

My mouth opened for a protest, but nothing came out. She was right. "I just want this to be done. I've had enough, even if that means letting him go."

She raised an eyebrow. The truth wasn't even plausible to her, but I was old. I was tired. How could I explain it to her? I didn't want to die. That was plain and simple what was happening. At this final hour, facing my greatest enemy, I turned into a damn coward. The boy could walk away. After all the twisted, destructive things he'd done, he could go on his way. It grated against everything I'd ever believed. He was a force of war and a thumb in the eye of justice, but there I was, letting him go.

"I'll do it," he said.

Shit. "What did you say?"

"I'll turn off my limiters. You think I can't handle it, but I can. You think it'll slow me down, and maybe that's enough to give you an advantage." He brushed his fingertips against the sleek handle of his pistol. "It's not."

"Well," I said, glancing at Trish. "Let's do it then."

Trish put a hand on my shoulder, stopping me on my way back to my dueling position. I shrugged her off. There wasn't any backing down, and she ought to have understood it.

"Don't arrest her," I muttered to Trish.

She gave me a quizzical look.

"Rosa. Whatever she's done can't be so bad."

A hint of a smile crossed Trish's face. "You're way behind on that one. I decided not to pursue her right around the time she saved all our asses for the third time." The implications of the request must have sunk in, because Trish pressed her lips together. She'd seen me go into situation I didn't think I could win.

Francis stood facing me, still not in position for the duel. "There was a time when I was young," he said, his voice quavering a little like a desert mirage. "There was a time..."

His expression changed, twisting from the blank slack to a mask of pure rage.

Then it snapped back. "There was a time when I was young and I loved my mother very much."

"A boy never stops loving his mother," I said.

His expression twisted again, and his brow furrowed in confusion. When he spoke, the inflection in his voice almost sounded like music. "She was a terrible mother, but no matter how much it hurt, I continued to love her." His fists clenched until his knuckles went white and his jagged fingernails bit into his flesh. "She *hurt* us," he said. "When the sun sat high in the sky she tied me to a post like a goat. She put"—his body twitched—"put ghosts in my eyes."

I shot Trish a look, but she gave me a questioning expression. Ghosts didn't make much sense to me, but Francis talked with a feverish tone as if there weren't much sense left in him to give.

"Pa was a man held slave to his heart." Now, Francis's face stopped returning to his usual slack emotionless visage. He ground his teeth and the muscles of his face worked like snakes under his flesh. A frown creased his brow. "I've killed so many people," he said. He finally met my gaze. "*You've* killed so many people."

I rocked back on my heels. "More than my share," I said, the words choking me.

"How do you deal with it?"

For a long time I didn't have an answer. How could I? There wasn't some trick to dealing with all the lives I'd snuffed out. Nobody had the key to sleeping soundly at night knowing all the paths I'd ended. Some of those paths might have led to redemption. Maybe I'd killed the hero who would have stood up to Chester Goodwin. My bullet might have stopped the woman who could have ended the war before it started.

Finally, I said, "I don't," and that tasted as much like truth as anything. "I swallow it back like the poison it is."

But that wasn't enough for Francis. His eyes narrowed and he took a step back. "Let's do this then," he said, nervous energy twitching at his fingertips.

My own nervous energy made my limbs numb and my eyes dry. The noon sun beat down, and even though I'd lived my whole life under the brutal Texas heat, this felt hotter than ever. Hell had burned its way through the red rock and met the Texas sun with something like an alliance.

Francis took his place on the dueling ground, squaring off against me.

Trish stepped up to her judge's position.

"Wait!" Quin said. She dropped her shotgun and ran up, but Trish stopped her. "J.D., you can't do this."

"Quin," I said. "Sometimes honor makes us do things we'd

rather not. This is that line we don't cross. This duel is fair and square, especially now that Francis is all the way here. Maybe this won't end the way you want, but it'll end. That's what matters."

"Feuds are just people being stupid," Quin said. "Don't you get that? It's not honor that makes you do this. It's just a bad play."

That got my notice. I had been expecting her to say it was stupid. Honor made us do stupid things, and that was expected. A bad play, though? That was something else. "What?" I asked, lacking anything better.

On the train, the crow cocked its head, just as confused as I was.

"You run it up the middle, J.D.," Quin said, her voice quiet. "Every goddamn play. Even when it's fourth and twenty you run it up the middle, because you don't know any other plays. It's predictable."

"Quin," Francis said, his voice cracking.

"I quit," she said. "Screw this. I'm not on your side anymore, Francis. You're being an ass." She turned to me. "You too."

Francis's face twisted into a mask of rage. "You can't quit," he whispered. His fingers touched his pistol.

Francis and Quin both drew their weapons, pointing them at each other. Francis held a sleek black gun and Quin still had that small pistol. It was a joke against a man like Francis, but she'd be dead before she ever learned that lesson.

Trish had one pistol pointed at each of them, and I hadn't even seen her move.

And my gun was still solidly in its holster. Shit, I really was getting slow. I looked to Legs and Rosa, who held up Chester Goodwin between them. "You getting in on this?"

"Naw, we're good," said Legs.

"Quin," I said, pitching my voice low and calm. "Francis."

My heartbeat slammed in my chest, ticking off like it was the last seconds before midnight.

"Francis," I said, "You owe me a duel."

"She owes me her life," he said.

"She might," I said. "But not until I get my duel."

Slowly, and with the reluctance of a scolded toddler, Francis holstered his gun. Quin did the same, followed by Trish.

Trish said, "Shall we?"

"Run it up the middle?" I said.

"As always." Trish took up her spot again and raised one pistol to the sky. "You know the rules. When I fire, you fellas do your thing. Shoot early, and my next bullet finds a home in your skull."

Time slowed and my heartbeat thundered in my ears. The crow lifted from its perch to fly high in the sky, circling above us like it knew one of us would soon be food.

It was probably right.

23

———

In the end, when a man stands shoulder to shoulder with death—not the adrenaline-filled crapshoot of danger, but *certain* death—he sees his life as it truly was. With that final rush of wisdom and enlightenment, he can finally sense with white-hot intensity the regret in all his days. It's the quiet reflection at the bottom of a shot of whiskey and the exhilarating revelations in the first sunrise of spring. That moment before the great beyond shone with burning truth when all chance at redemption up and fled.

And in that moment, my only thought was that I hadn't actually done too bad. Sure, I'd failed more than I'd succeeded, but things came together when they mattered. I might not have been right all the time, but I'd always managed to point my stubborn self in the direction that seemed best at the time. In the end, there weren't any points for effort, but effort's all we get.

Those last few seconds, my body stretched past the pains of life. The searing aches that had settled so deep into my bones left me acutely aware of every one of those final breaths. Old age sloughed off and all the aches that had plagued me flew away into the wind. My palms dried and my muscles tensed, ready to pounce like a cat.

Francis narrowed his eyes. He was fast. No doubt he'd move quicker than any man I'd ever drawn against. He had long since abandoned the limitations of baseline human. His nerves were a tightly optimized machine, and my only chance at stopping that coiled snake lay in the foolish idea that his rampaging emotions might hinder him.

They wouldn't.

That man hated me. I saw it clear in his eyes. He had hated me since before I stopped his plan to subjugate Texas. He despised me all these long years. Hell, his hatred sprang up before I'd ever killed his mama, and he had every right to continue on hating me until the day I died.

Today.

He had every right to hate me until today.

Quin stood, petrified with the horror of what we were doing. Mutual murder, that's what it was. Agreed-upon rules for the destruction of human life. All in the name of honor.

The quarterback was right. I was running up the middle just like I always had. Where else was there to run? Violence had always been my go-to play. I first stepped into the Texas wild to do violence, and I'd never stopped. Not as a ranger in the Civil War, not as a lawman, not as a bounty hunter. Maybe I'd tried other plays. My past was riddled with failed attempts to avoid bloodshed.

Deep down in my gut I believed that sometimes bloodshed was necessary. Only, I always happened to be around when it was. It wasn't that I brought violence to the wilds of Texas.

Violence brought me.

My nerves sizzled. Something far grimmer than hope pulsed through my veins. Maybe I would end Francis before he killed me.

But no. Killing Francis didn't solve anything. Deep down in

my bones I knew that wasn't the answer. Only one of us would walk off that impromptu dueling ground, and it sure as hell wasn't going to be me.

Trish fired her gun, and my movement superseded thought. Fingers touched the pistol. Drew it.

Aimed.

I'd beaten him. In that sliver of a second between her shot and his, I had my chance. One fraction of a moment to run up the middle. Violence, like I'd always done.

Point the pistol. Fire.

But I didn't take it. The Red Number Five stayed in that chamber, all potential and no action.

Because Francis wasn't the monster I'd always made him out to be, and technology wasn't the poison slowly killing our society. The poison was the people not caring enough to make a change. If there was one thing Francis had, it was the stubborn will to make a difference. His actions were monstrous, and his ethics were bankrupt—but everything he did was an attempt to fix a broken world. Can he help that the shattered system produced a shattered boy?

The gun tumbled from my hand, which had gone inexplicably numb.

Then I heard Francis's gunshot.

I brought my hand in front of me and tried to puzzle out what had happened. Why wasn't it working?

Quin caught me when I dropped to my knees. She shouted something, but her words were a jumble in my head. Blood covered her hands. Her poncho. Trish knelt next to her, and she touched my face. Her hand was cool and warm all at once and surprisingly gentle.

My chest, right over my heart. Francis had shot me in the heart.

Time doesn't pass without a heartbeat. Silence thundered in the back of my skull for eternity.

Francis knelt in front of me, tears streaming down his face. "I'm sorry," he said. "I'm so sorry. You had the shot. Why didn't you take the shot?"

I opened my mouth to speak, but no words came out.

Behind Francis, I saw Chester Goodwin pull himself up against the wreckage next to him. He lurched forward on ruined legs, and rage burned in his eyes.

Chester raised a pistol at Francis. It shook in his bloody hand. That was my blood on his hand, and I understood what he meant about Francis choosing me. I had the final dose of Reginald's bioweapon. It had been fighting my mechanical parts since the moment Francis had scratched me on the Yellowstone crater.

Goodwin opened his mouth to say something.

I never gave him the chance to form another word. Acting on impulse, I snatched up my revolver and fired. The Red Number Five exploded like a mule kick, shattering the bones in my thankfully numb hand. Chester's head cracked in a spray of bone and brain, and his corpse hit the earth.

Francis didn't even flinch.

"I'm sorry," I said, voice so quiet he might not have heard.

He knelt down, plucked something from my pocket, and placed it at the base of my neck where the metal of my arm met my flesh. "That's all I ever wanted."

"I forgive you," I said with my last breath.

A pulse ran down my spine and tingled in my metal arm. I knew that feeling. It was the subsonic thrum of an e-cuff. Every mechanical part of me shut down, from my big arm to the nanomachines pulsing through my blood.

Then everything went black.

24

The white room wasn't much to look at, but that didn't bother me much since I was too busy being shocked at the fact I was doing any looking at all. Confused, I lay there wearing nothing but a hospital robe and a week-old beard. I smelled ripe, but the sheets were clean and when I reached out to press the call button, I noticed something else.

My metal arm was missing.

Better part of the shoulder was missing, scarred over with silver-white flesh. My whole body felt light with that burden gone. The constant ache of my adult life had faded into the mild numbness of old age. My heart beat. It beat!

"They said you'd wake up," Quin said from somewhere behind me, "but I didn't believe them."

I twisted to get a look at her, but the movement caused a cascade of sharp pains to run the length of my chest. The missing space where my metal arm used to be flared with what must have been imaginary pain.

Quin circled the bed and took hold of my one hand. Her fingers felt tiny in my calloused palm. "Don't try to talk, old man." Her voice hitched, but she swallowed it back. "You're messed up real good. They say your heart healed fast enough it started working before you were really dead."

"Healed?" Ow. I shouldn't have tried to talk.

She smiled, but her eyes seemed sad. "That bug Reginald was working on really works. It healed you. Those people on the train? They were guinea pigs for him to experiment on."

Reginald. That sick bastard really had used Casket Jones's bioengineered virus to make something new. Goodwin must have wanted it to control his people. It granted powerful healing, but with an incompatibility with other tech. It'd be a perfect way to produce workers with incredible endurance and an inability to garner the kind of technological sophistication needed for a true rebellion.

Well, I'd never been much good with tech, anyway.

Quin must have seen my questioning look. "Far as they can tell, you won't get the tumors Casket Jones had to deal with. You should be fine once you've had some time to recover."

But how? When had I gotten infected? I pulled my hand from Quin and looked at the white scar where Francis had scratched me. He'd administered the dose right when I'd first captured him. That one scratch severed my ties with tech and saved my life all in one swipe.

"Did you know?" I whispered. Speaking still hurt, but I had to know.

"I don't think anyone really knows what goes through that guy's head. He told me to stick with you, so I did."

My expression prompted her to continue.

"I wasn't lying when I said I wanted to get out of town." She hesitated before continuing. "I owed him."

"Francis has a habit of generating debt." The more I spoke the less each word hurt. Maybe a lesser side effect of what the prisoners on the train experienced.

"It's not like that." She gave my hand a squeeze. "He stopped my mama." She swallowed, and for several long seconds I thought she might not continue. "He stopped her from killing my pa. It was bad all around, but Francis stopped her. Got her help. It was one of those things that brews for years, you know? People are like that sometimes."

I let out a breath I hadn't known I was holding. Something tense lingered in that room between us. "Nobody saved Francis's family," I finally said. "But it should have been me."

She stayed silent for a long while, and eventually the fog of exhaustion rolled back over me. I tried to hang on, understanding that I probably wouldn't see Quin again when I woke. It didn't do much good.

Just before my eyelids became too heavy to keep up, she said, "He forgives you."

I drifted off to the first decent sleep I'd had in years.

There was a spot in Dead Oak across from the tavern where the people always passed in good cheer. This was my spot, and for almost a year, I made my retirement there greeting folks with the tip of a hat and a crooked smile. Some were the long-time residents of Dead Oak. Others were folks recovering from Reginald's strange experiments. After we'd rescued them from the train, many had stuck around, not wanting to return to their hard lives at the edge of the Yellowstone Caldera. Some stayed mute, but many didn't. All of them rejected tech implants and augmentations. It was almost like having a town full of like-minded individuals. Trish came by to visit often enough. I like to think it was because she'd grown fond of me, but more likely it was because my spot was just down the street from her Sheriff's office.

Hazel Brown was dark as her mama and more rebellious than her pa ever dreamed. At a year old, she never sat, never stilled, and never spent much time on any one lap in a gathering —except mine. She'd sit and listen to my stories for an hour if I told them, and that day Abi and Ben had left her while they went for a ride through town on errands.

"I rode that bull till it fell over," I said in my best storytelling voice.

Hazel ran a hand along the white stubble on my chin and gave me a disbelieving look.

"I'm dead serious, young lady. Rode it to the ground. Didn't know at the time it had a chip on its head making it fight even harder, but I stayed put anyway."

"Nobody's going to believe that story," Ben said, riding the skittish black gelding. It wasn't skittish for him.

"You were there!"

Abi, atop her chestnut mare, rode alongside Ben. She dismounted and Hazel jumped off my lap to run to her. "Telling tall stories again, J.D.?"

Trish looked good as ever when she rolled out of the station. She came up to me with swagger in her step and a smile on her face. "Always," she said.

I tipped my hat. "Sheriff."

"Funny how you're always here," she said.

I stuck a thumb out at the little domed building where I'd made my home. "I live here."

"True." She rested, hand on hip. "Say, you wouldn't be able to find some time to help a lady out, would you?"

I pursed my lips. "Might be able to work something out, so long as it isn't heavy lifting."

Trish said, "Gerald and Rosa ran into a little trouble yesterday. They handled it, but it sounds like there might be a new gang in town."

"Who the hell is Gerald?"

"Legs."

Huh. Hadn't known that. "They have that kid yet?"

"On the way," Abi said, hoisting Hazel up onto her hip. "Twins, I hear."

That put a smile on my lips. Legs would make a decent go at being a father, but twins might be a bit much. "Well, if you see them, tell them I'm a fair hand at changing diapers, even one-handed."

She pulled out my old gun belt, complete with my own revolver. "Could use a deputy, old man." The belt hung there in her hand like a dead snake. "We have a lead on finally tracking down Reginald."

"Might be you can find someone younger to deputize."

"Sure," she said. "But I'd be hard pressed to find someone better."

"Abi's better," I said.

"She helped me out last week."

"Sunset?"

"I don't mix business and pleasure."

The scorched Texas air tasted like dust on my lips. I glanced at Abi and Ben, then at little Hazel. "I'm not in that business anymore." I nodded to my missing arm. "All the advantages are gone now, and I'm old to boot." I didn't want to say that I'd lost my sense for justice. Ever since Goodwin's War ended, I'd been reluctant to even pick up a pistol for fear of setting off something even worse.

"Frank is doing well," Ben said, mercifully changing the subject. "Keeps himself isolated a bit much, but he's really starting to improve."

There was a time I'd wanted him dead. Now Francis William Brown—Frank—stayed in house arrest on the Brown Ranch. They'd isolated his tech—burned out his nodes and switched off anything that might make him a danger. He'd agreed to it too, which was one more sign that he didn't really deserve the fate he'd been given. He never had.

"We're all doing our best," I said. "He beat me fair and square."

"That's one way of seeing it." Trish pulled the gun belt back.

"Or it could be that your act of mercy showed him how to be better."

"I've got a good life here," I said. "Got Muffin out back to care for, and I've got friends now. We play cards most days. There's even a fella I got my eye on, if you don't mind me saying."

"Emberton Smith?" Abi asked.

"How'd you know that?"

"You're a damn flirt, J.D. Everyone knows that."

"Huh." I scratched my stubbly beard. It had gone full white, but still came in strong. "Point is, there's more to life than chasing fools."

Trish nodded. "Yet here I am."

With that, she turned to leave. The high noon sun glinted off the sleek steel of her two guns. She was the best sheriff Dead Oak ever had. Maybe the best to grace all of Texas. Trish could have stopped me from dueling Francis. The whole thing could have played out differently.

It didn't, because Trish's sense of justice was so much better than mine ever had been. She had the kind of honor that burned in a heart the way coals burn long after a campfire's died down. Trish glowed with it, and in that heat others burst into flame.

I stood from my comfortable spot across from the tavern. "Hold up," I said.

She turned and raised an eyebrow at me.

"Give me the damn gun," I said.

Trish tossed the belt, gun and all, across the dusty Texas street. I caught it as I descended the steps from my home.

Together, we made our way down the center of Dead Oak, justice in our minds, peace in our sights, and honor in our hearts.

ACKNOWLEDGMENTS

The list of people I'd like to thank for helping me get Honor in an Age of Metal and Men off the ground is too long for me to ever fully comprehend, so I'll just throw a few out there and hope I don't make anyone too terribly angry at being left out. My wife Carol, of course, gets first billing in all things. Without her support I couldn't get much of anything done. Isaac and Gabe, the best sons a father could ever hope for, might not have pushed me to write this book, but they give my writing inspiration every single day. The members of the Rochester Writers Group has always been a great support for me. Fellow Rochester writers Mike Kalmbach, K. Bird Lincoln, J. Lynn Else, Ben Green, Krista Street, and Brian Smith are always challenging me to do better.

Honor in an Age of Metal and Men was a long time coming, plotted out in my brain since the very beginning of Justice. It sat there for a long time, waiting for the opportunity to spring forth. I finally had some time between other projects in February of 2019, and decided to make a go of it. The first draft was completed that month, and the dozens of rounds of edits happened over the course of the following summer. It's a much more efficient process than what I stumbled through with Justice in an Age of Metal and Men, and I'm quite happy with how the whole series comes together as a whole. I hope you all are, too.

BIN TRAVERLER FORM

Cut By: _Johandri Ascanio_ Qty _21_ Date _07-30-26_

Scanned By:_______________________Qty________Date____________

Scanned Batch ID's

_______________ _______________ _______________

Notes / Exceptions

____